Cesar was losing it. He knew he was losing it. But he couldn't take his mouth off Lexie's. He'd never tasted anything so sweet. Or so wicked. The way that lush mouth softened under his, the feel of that body under his hands...

Dios.

Cesar finally pulled back, heart hammering. He did not ravish women in the back of his cars. He was cool, calm, controlled. Right now he felt anything but. He could hardly see straight. His body was on fire.

Lexie was looking at him with huge eyes. She thought he'd done that on purpose. And he had—but not for the reasons she obviously suspected. He wanted to make sure there was no ambiguity about how he felt about her.

He cupped that delicate jaw. Her mouth was pink, swollen. He couldn't help running his thumb across that pouting lower lip, feeling its fleshy softness.

'Make no mistake, Lexie, I want you...and not just to distract the crowds. You know the truth of what I said earlier. We will be lovers for real.'

BLOOD BROTHERS

Power and passion run in their veins

Rafaele and Alexio have learned that to feel emotion is to be weak. Calculated ruthlessness brings them immense success in the boardroom and in the bedroom. But a storm is coming with the sudden appearance of a long-lost half-brother, Cesar, and three women who will change their lives for ever...

*Read **Rafaele Falcone's** story in:*
WHEN FALCONE'S WORLD STOPS TURNING
February 2014

*Read **Alexio Christakos's** story in:*
WHEN CHRISTAKOS MEETS HIS MATCH
April 2014

*And read **Cesar Da Silva's** story in:*
WHEN DA SILVA BREAKS THE RULES
June 2014

WHEN DA SILVA
BREAKS THE RULES

BY
ABBY GREEN

Published in Great Britain 2014
by Mills & Boon, an imprint of Harlequin (UK) Limited,
Eton House, 18-24 Paradise Road, Richmond, Surrey, TW9 1SR

© 2014 Abby Green

ISBN: 978 0 263 24233 1

Abby Green spent her teens reading Mills & Boon® romances. She then spent many years working in the film and TV industry as an assistant director. One day while standing outside an actor's trailer in the rain, she thought: *There has to be more than this.* So she sent off a partial to Mills & Boon®. After many rewrites they accepted her first book and an author was born. She lives in Dublin, Ireland, and you can find out more here: www.abby-green.com

Recent titles by the same author:

WHEN CHRISTAKOS MEETS HIS MATCH
  (Blood Brothers)
WHEN FALCONE'S WORLD STOPS TURNING
  (Blood Brothers)
FORGIVEN BUT NOT FORGOTTEN?
EXQUISITE REVENGE

**Did you know these are also available as eBooks?
Visit www.millsandboon.co.uk**

PROLOGUE

CESAR DA SILVA hated to admit that coming here had had any effect on him, but his gut was heavy and tight as he stood on the path near the grave. He asked himself again why he'd even come and reflexively his fingers closed around the small velvet pouch with its heavy weight in his hand. He'd almost forgotten about it.

He smiled cynically. Who would have thought that at the age of thirty-seven he'd be obeying urges and compulsions? Usually he was the king of logic and reason.

People drifted away from the open grave a short distance across the hilly green space. Ornate mini-mausoleum-style headstones dotted the cemetery in the hills of Athens, its grass no doubt kept generously watered in the Greek heat.

Finally there were only two men left by the grave. Both tall, of similar height, with dark hair. One had slightly darker and shorter hair than the other. They were broad, as Cesar was, with powerful builds.

It was no wonder they were all similar. He was their half-brother. And they had no idea he even existed. He saw one put his hand on the shoulder of the other. They were Rafaele Falcone and Alexio Christakos. They all shared the same mother, but had different fathers.

Cesar waited for icy rage to surge upwards upon seeing this evidence of the family he'd always been denied, but instead he felt a kind of aching emptiness. They came towards him then, talking in quiet voices. Cesar caught his youngest half-brother's words on the slight breeze—something like, *'Couldn't even clean up for the funeral...?'*

Falcone replied indistinctly, with a quirk to his mouth, and Christakos riposted, smiling too.

The emptiness receded and anger rose up within Cesar. But it was a different kind of anger. These men were joking, joshing, just feet away from their mother's grave. And since when did Cesar feel protective of the woman who had taught him from the age of three that he could depend on no one?

Galvanised by that very unwelcome revelation, Cesar moved forward and Falcone looked up, words dying on his lips, smile fading. Falcone's gaze was enquiring at first and then, as Cesar drilled holes into him with his stare, it became something else. Cold.

With a quick flick of a glance to the younger man by his half-brother's side, Cesar noted that they'd also all inherited varying shades of their beautiful but treacherous mother's green eyes.

'May we help you?' Falcone asked coolly.

Cesar glanced over them both again and then at the open grave in the distance. He asked, with a derisive curl to his lip, 'Are there any more of us?'

Falcone looked at Christakos, who was frowning, and said, '*Us?* What are you talking about?'

Cesar pushed down the spreading blackness within him and said with ominous quiet, 'You don't remember, do you?'

But he could see from the dawning shock that his half-brother did, and Cesar didn't like the way something inside him tightened at that recognition. Those light green eyes widened imperceptibly. He paled.

Cesar's voice was rough in the still, quiet air. 'She brought you to my home—you must have been nearly three, and I was almost seven. She wanted to take me with her then, but I wouldn't leave. Not after she'd abandoned me.'

In a slightly hoarse voice Falcone asked, 'Who *are* you?'

Cesar smiled, but it didn't meet his eyes. 'I'm your older brother—*half-brother*. My name is Cesar Da Silva. I came today to pay my respects to the woman who gave me life...not that she deserved it. I was curious to see if any more would crawl out of the woodwork, but it looks like it's just us.'

Christakos erupted. 'What the *hell*—?'

Cesar cast him a cold glance. Somewhere deep down he felt a twinge of conscience for imparting the news like this, on this day. But then he recalled the long, aching years of dark loneliness, knowing that these two men had *not* been abandoned, and crushed it ruthlessly.

Falcone still looked slightly shell-shocked. He gestured to his half-brother. 'This is Alexio Christakos...our younger brother.'

Cesar knew exactly who he was—who they both were. He'd always known. Because his grandparents had made sure he'd known every single little thing about them. He bit out, 'Three brothers by three fathers...and yet she didn't abandon either of *you* to the wolves.'

He stepped forward then, and Alexio stepped forward too. The two men stood almost nose to nose, Cesar topping his youngest brother in height only by an inch.

He gritted out, 'I didn't come here to fight you, brother. I have no issue with either of you.' *Liar*, a small voice chided.

Alexio's mouth thinned, 'Only with our dead mother, *if* what you say is true.'

Cesar smiled, but it was bitter. 'Oh, it's true all right—more's the pity.' He stepped around Alexio then, before either man could see the rise of an emotion he couldn't name, and walked to the open grave.

He took the velvet pouch out of his pocket and dropped it down into the dark space, where it fell onto the coffin with a hollow thud. In the pouch was a very old silver medallion featuring the patron saint of bullfighters: San Pedro Regalado.

Even now the bitter memory was vivid. His mother was in a black suit, hair drawn back, Her features as exquisitely beautiful as any he'd ever seen. Eyes raw from crying. She'd taken the medallion from where it hung around her neck on a piece of worn rope and had put it around his neck. She had tucked it under his shirt and said, *'He will protect you, Cesar. Because I can't at the moment. Don't ever take it off. And I promise I will come back for you soon.'*

But she hadn't come back. Not for a long time. And when she finally had it had been too late. Something had withered and died inside him. *Hope.*

Cesar had taken off the medallion the night he'd let that hope die. He'd been six years old. He'd known then that nothing could protect him except himself. She deserved to have the medallion back now—he'd had no need of it for a long time.

Eventually Cesar turned and walked back to where his half-brothers were still standing, faces inscrutable. He might have smiled, if he'd been able, to recognise this familiar trait. An ache gripped him in the region of his chest where he knew his heart should be. But as he knew well, and as he'd been told numerous times by angry lovers, he had no heart.

After a taut silence Cesar knew he had nothing to say to these men. These strangers. He didn't even feel envy any more. He felt empty.

He turned and got into the back of his car and curtly instructed his driver to go. It was done. He'd said goodbye to his mother, which was more than she'd ever deserved, and if there was one tiny piece of his soul that hadn't shrivelled up by now then maybe it could be saved.

CHAPTER ONE

Castillo Da Silva, near Salamanca

CESAR WAS HOT, sweaty, grimy and thoroughly disgruntled. All he wanted was a cold shower and a stiff drink. A punishing ride around his vast estate on his favourite stallion had failed to put a dent in the dark cloud that had clung to him since his return that afternoon from his half-brother Alexio's wedding in Paris. Those scenes of chirpy happiness still grated on his soul.

It also irritated him intensely that he'd given in to the rogue compulsion to go.

As he neared the stables his black mood increased on seeing the evidence of a serious breach of his privacy. A film was due to start shooting on his estate after the weekend, for the next four weeks. If that wasn't bad enough, the stars, director and producers were all staying *in* the *castillo*.

He wasn't unaware of his complicated relationship to his home. It was both prison and sanctuary. But one thing was sure: Cesar hated his privacy being invaded like this.

Huge equipment trucks lined his driveway. People were wandering about holding clipboards, speaking into walkie talkies. A massive marquee had been set up, where locals from the nearby town were being decked out as extras in nineteenth-century garb.

All that was missing was a circus tent with flags flying and a clown outside saying, *Roll up! Roll up!*

One of his biggest stable yards had been cleared out so that they could use it as the unit base. The unit base, as a film assistant had explained earnestly to Cesar, was where the actors got ready every day and where the crew would eat. As if he cared!

But he'd feigned interest for the benefit of his friend Juan Cortez, who was the Lord Mayor of Villaporto, the local town, and the reason why Cesar had given this idea even half a second's consideration. They'd been friends since the age of ten, when they'd both had to admit defeat during a fist fight or remain fighting till dawn and lose all their teeth. And they would have—both were stubborn enough.

As his friend had pointed out, 'Nearly everyone has been employed in some capacity—accommodation, catering, locations, the art department. Even my mother is involved in making clothes for the extras and putting up some of the crew. I haven't seen her so excited in years.'

Cesar couldn't fail to acknowledge the morale and economic boost the film had already brought to the locale. He was known in the press for his ruthless dealings with people and businesses—one journalist had likened his methods to those of the cold, dead-eyed shark before it ate you whole. But Cesar wasn't completely heartless—especially if it involved his own local community.

More than one person caught a glimpse of his glowering features and looked away hurriedly, but Cesar was oblivious, already figuring out how he could rearrange his schedule to make sure he was away for as much of the next four weeks as possible.

To his relief, his own private stable yard, which was strictly off-limits to the crew, was empty when he returned. He wasn't in the mood to deal with anyone—not even a groom. After unsaddling his horse and hosing him down, Cesar led him back to his stall and made sure he was secure, patting his still quivering flesh after their exertion.

It was only when he was turning to leave again that Cesar spotted a movement out of the corner of his eye and turned to look.

And stopped breathing, and thinking.

In the other corner of the quiet stable stood a woman. Cesar felt slightly dizzy for a moment and wondered if he was seeing an apparition.

She was wearing a white corset that cinched in her waist to almost impossible proportions while provocatively pushing up the abundant swells of her breasts. Long wavy golden hair was pulled back from an ethereally beautiful face and left to tumble down her back. Very feminine hips curved out from that tiny waist and a long, voluminous skirt almost touched the ground.

She was stunning...exquisite. She was Venus incarnate. She couldn't be real. Nothing so perfect existed in reality.

Almost without realising that he was moving, Cesar closed the distance between them. She didn't move. Just stared at him, looking as transfixed as he felt. Imbuing the moment with an even headier other-worldly feeling.

Her eyes were huge and blue...piercing. She was tiny, and it seemed to call to some deep, primal part of him. Evoking an alien urge to protect.

Her face was small and heart-shaped, but with an inherent strength that elevated it out of the merely beautiful to the extraordinary. High cheekbones. Elegant straight nose. A full, lush mouth made for sin and sinners. Skin like alabaster.

There was a beauty spot close to the edge of her upper lip. She exuded an earthy and very feminine sexual allure. She couldn't be real. Yet every single ounce of his masculinity was humming and throbbing in reaction to her luminosity.

As if to check that he wasn't losing it completely, Cesar reached out a hand, noting with almost dispassionate surprise that it trembled slightly. He cupped his hand near her cheek and jaw, without actually touching her, almost afraid that she might disappear if he did...

And then he touched her...and she didn't disappear. She was *real*. Warm. Skin as soft as silk.

A movement made his eyes drop and he saw her chest moving up and down rapidly with her breaths.

'*Dios,*' he said faintly, almost to himself, 'you are real.'

Her mouth opened. Cesar saw small, even white teeth. Her tongue-tip pink. She said, 'I...' and then stopped.

Just that one tiny word had been uttered in a husky voice, making Cesar's whole body tighten with a need that was unprecedented.

Sliding his fingers further around her jaw to the back of her neck, silky hair tickling his hand, Cesar tugged her into him and after a minute hesitation she came, stumbling ever so slightly. All he knew, once he felt the barest whisper of a touch of her body to his, was that he couldn't hold back now even if a thousand men tried to stop him.

He lowered his head and his mouth touched hers, and all that sweet, soft voluptuousness pierced him right to the centre of his being, and threw him into the pit of a fire of lust so strong it obliterated everything he knew, or thought he knew.

Cesar felt her hands clutching at him, grabbing his shirt. Any resistance vanished when her mouth opened under his, and his arms tightened around her as his hungry tongue thrust into that hot, moist cavern.

However sweet that first initial taste had been, it turned to pure sin. Decadent and rich. Her tongue was sharp and smooth, teasing. Stoking his levels of arousal so that every bit of blood seemed to be rushing to the centre of his body, making that shaft of flesh lengthen and stiffen painfully.

Moving his hands to her waist, encircling it, Cesar almost groaned aloud when he felt his fingers meet. That evidence of her intense femininity pushed his body over the edge, made it betray him as if he were an over-sexed teenager.

He could feel her chest, struggling with constricted breath, moving up and down rapidly. Blood surging anew, Cesar lifted a hand and dragged it up between their bodies, itching to touch that smooth pale skin.

When he came into contact with the swell of one breast his body pulsed with a need that shocked him. He broke the contact of their mouths for a moment, resting his forehead against hers, overwhelmed at the strength of his desire.

'Please…'

Her voice sounded even huskier…needy. The way he felt. He needed this woman *now*. Needed to free himself and lift up her skirts and plunge right into the centre of that taut, smooth body. To feel her legs wrap around him.

On some very dim and distant level Cesar was aware that he had become animalistic. Reduced to the cravings and needs of a base animal in an effort to achieve a kind of satisfaction he'd never anticipated before.

But that still couldn't stop him. Not after that husky *please* had filled the space between them.

Branding her mouth with his again, the kiss was open-mouthed and carnal. Electrifying.

In the act of lifting up her skirts, almost desperate now, Cesar jerked and flinched when a flash of light seemed to illuminate the world for a second. Like the crack of a whip. Shattering the heady moment.

Lifting his head from where their mouths were welded together, Cesar could only see two huge pools of blue, ringed by long black lashes. That plump mouth was pink. He could feel her chest moving against his.

Then there was another flash, and a rapid jarring, clicking sound. He flinched again. Some vague notion of reality and sanity returned from a long distance. He turned his head, but it was the hardest thing to do—to look away from that face. Those eyes.

He saw a man standing at the entrance of the stables holding a camera up to his face. It was the equivalent of having a bucket of cold water thrown over him. Suddenly reality was back.

Cesar straightened up. Instinctively he pushed the woman behind him as he snarled at the man who was backing away, still shooting, 'Get out of here. *Now.*' One of Cesar's grooms appeared near the door and he rapped out at him, 'Get Security now—and get that man's camera.'

But the photographer had disappeared, and even though Cesar's groom darted away after him Cesar had the sinking feeling it would be too late. He'd reacted too late himself.

Becoming aware of rapid harsh breathing behind him, Cesar turned around.

And almost fell into the pit again when he saw those huge blue eyes staring up at him and that body which made him ache.

But reality had intruded. This woman was no apparition or ghost. She was flesh and blood, and he had just lost his legendary control spectacularly. *Dios*, had he gone mad?

Accusingly, Cesar asked, 'Who the hell *are* you?'

Lexie Anderson was barely aware of the sharp accusation in the deep, deliciously accented voice. She couldn't seem to get enough breath into her challenged lungs to speak. All she could ask herself was: *what the hell had just happened?*

She remembered wandering away from the camera tests

while they set up the lights and finding these quiet stables.
She loved horses, so she had come in to investigate.

Then the peace had been shattered when this man had
appeared in the courtyard on a huge black stallion. He'd
swung down off the horse's back and from that moment
on everything had got a little hazy.

Lexie had been mesmerised by his powerful physique
and the play of muscles under his close-fitting polo top and
jodhpurs as he'd tended to the horse. And that had been
before she'd seen his face properly. When he'd heard her
and turned around.

He was stunning. Beautiful. But with a masculine edge
that made 'beautiful' sound too...pretty. He was hard.
Edgy. Dark. Messy dark blond hair. A sensually sculpted
mouth surrounded by stubble shadowing a very masculine jaw.

But it was his eyes that rendered Lexie a bit stupid
and mute even now, as he waited for her reply. They were
green—unusual and stark against dark olive skin. Not
hazel, or golden, or light green. Something between all
three. Unnerving. Mesmerising.

And he smelled of *man*. Sweat and musk and heat.
Along with something tangy. Woodsy.

Lexie shook her head, as if that might make all this
disappear. Maybe she was having some bizarre dream.
Because she knew that what had just happened was unprecedented. She did not react to complete strangers by
letting them kiss her, or by feeling as if she'd die if they
didn't *keep* kissing her.

She remembered his big hands around her waist, then
reaching under her skirts to pull them up, and how she'd
burned between her legs for him to touch her there.

Now was most definitely *not* the time to be assimilat-
ing that cataclysmic information.

'I'm...' She stopped, her tongue feeling heavy in her

mouth. She tried again. 'I'm Lexie Anderson. I'm with the film.'

Lexie's face burned when she realised exactly how she was dressed, and how this man's eyes had widened when he'd seen her. Belatedly self-conscious, she went to cross her arms but realised the corset only made things worse—especially when those green eyes dropped to her heaving flesh again.

Feeling trapped now—literally backed into a corner—and not liking it, Lexie forced her legs to move, wobbly as they were, and stepped cautiously around him.

He turned to face her. Eyes cool, unreadable. Hands clenched into fists by his sides. 'You're Lexie Anderson... the lead actress?'

She nodded.

He looked at her, his eyes no longer unreadable now. Angry. 'And how did you get in here?'

She blinked, not understanding for a moment. 'I didn't see any sign or a gate...I just saw the horses—'

'It's off-limits here. You should leave—now.'

Anger gripped Lexie. She'd just behaved in a way that was completely out of character. The last thing she needed was to feel the lash of *his* censure. Stiffly, she replied, 'I didn't realise this was off-limits. If you can tell me how to get back to the unit base, I'll happily leave.'

His voice was harsh, curt. 'Turn left. It's at the end of the lane and to your right.'

Seething inwardly now, because she had been overcome by the first rush of physical desire she'd ever felt, and it had been for some anonymous person who worked at the castle and not even someone she *knew* or who was particularly charming, Lexie stalked off, tense as a board.

Then she heard the man curse and he commanded, 'Wait. Stop.'

Lexie stopped, breathing hard, and turned reluctantly again, rigid with tension.

He walked towards her, his movements powerfully agile, and she stepped back. His eyes flashed but she just tipped up her chin. What was wrong with her judgement? There wasn't anything remotely forgiving or alluring about this man. He was all hard edges and brooding energy.

He looked grim. 'That was a paparazzo. He got our picture.'

She'd forgotten. Her brain was refusing to work properly. Lexie could feel her blood draining south. The man must have feared she was about to faint or something, because he took her arm and none too gently drew her over to a haystack by the entrance, where he all but pushed her down onto it.

She ripped her arm free and glared up at him, hating the betraying quiver in her belly at his touch. 'There's no need to manhandle me. I'm perfectly fine.'

As if to confirm her worst suspicions, the young groom came running back, his face red.

'Well?' barked the man.

Lexie felt like standing up and telling him to go and take out his aggression on someone his own size, but she was disgusted to feel that her legs might not hold her up.

'Señor Da Silva…'

The groom spoke quickly after that, in incomprehensible Spanish, but Lexie was now gaping at the tall, angry man who was answering equally gutturally and quickly, making the groom turn puce and rush off again.

Lexie was too shocked to care for the groom's welfare any more. He turned back to her and she said faintly, 'You're Cesar Da Silva…?'

'Yes.'

He didn't seem to be too thrilled she'd made the connection. She'd thought he was a worker! Lexie hadn't recognised him as the owner of this entire estate because he was famously reclusive. Also, she'd never expected *the* Cesar Da Silva to be so young and gorgeous.

She had to will down her mortification when she thought of how she'd been all but crawling all over him like a hungry little kitten only minutes before. Begging. *'Please.'*

Oh, God.

She stood up. She had to get out of here. This was not her. She'd been invaded by some kind of body-snatcher.

'Where do you think you're going?'

Lexie looked at him. Anger flashed up again—at him and herself. She put her hands on her hips. 'You just told me to leave, didn't you? So I'm leaving.'

She moved around him again, towards the entrance, relieved that her legs were working.

'Wait.'

Lexie stopped and sighed heavily, turned around. She arched a brow, hiding how damn intimidating she thought he was. 'What now?'

He couldn't have looked more stern. 'That photographer got away. My groom saw him get into a car before any of the security guards could be alerted. I would imagine that right about now he's emailing pictures of us to any number of agencies around the world.'

Lexie felt sick. She felt even sicker to think that she was potentially going to be splashed across the tabloids *again*. And with Cesar Da Silva, one of the most reclusive billionaires in the world. It would be a sensation and it was the last thing she needed—*more* intense media interest.

She bit her lip. 'This isn't good.'

'No,' Da Silva agreed, 'it's not. I have no desire to become the centre of some grubby little tabloid sensation.'

Lexie glared at him, incensed. 'Well, neither do I.' She pointed a finger at him. 'And *you* kissed *me*.'

'You didn't stop me,' he shot back. 'And what were you doing in here anyway?'

Lexie burned. No, she hadn't stopped him. Anything but. She'd been caught up in a dreamlike state of...hot insanity.

'I told you.' Her voice was stiff, with the full ramifications of what had happened sinking in. 'I saw the stables, I wanted to see the horses... We're doing camera tests with Make-up and Wardrobe, and while they were setting up the lighting...'

She tensed as realisation hit.

'The camera tests! I have to go back—they'll be looking for me.'

Lexie went to rush off, but her arm was caught by a big hand. She turned and gritted her jaw. Those green eyes were like burning gems in his spectacular face. His hand on her arm was hot.

'This isn't over—'

Just then a PA rushed into the yard, breathless. 'Lexie, *there* you are. We've been looking all over for you. They're ready to shoot again.'

Lexie pulled free of Cesar Da Silva's grip. She could see his irritation at the interruption but she was glad, needing to get away from his disturbing presence and so she could try to assimilate what had just happened.

Lexie tore her gaze from his and hurried after the officious PA, who was speaking into the walkie-talkie microphone that came out of her sleeve near her wrist. Lexie heard her saying, 'Found her...coming now...one minute...'

Her head was reeling. She felt as if in the space of just that last...fifteen minutes?...her entire world had been altered in some very fundamental way.

She'd let that man...who had been a complete stranger... walk up to her and kiss her. Without a second's hesitation. And not just kiss her...*devour* her. And she'd kissed him back.

She could still feel that dizzying, rushing sweep of desire like a wave through her body. Impossible to ignore or deny. Immediate. All-consuming.

It was crazy, but she'd felt protected by his much larger bulk when he'd put her behind him as soon as he'd seen the paparazzo. Lexie wasn't used to feeling tiny, or in need of protection, even though she *was* physically small at five foot two. She'd been standing up for herself for so long now that she wasn't usually taken unawares in a situation like that. It sent a shiver of unease through her.

The photographer.

She felt sick again. Memories of lurid headlines and pictures rose up. Before she could dwell on it though, they'd entered the yard where the camera tests were taking place and everyone snapped to attention as soon as she appeared.

The cameraman beckoned her over. 'Right, Lexie, we need you over here on your mark, please.'

Cesar paced back and forth in his office, behind his desk. If it were at all possible his black mood had just become even blacker. Like a living, seething thing crackling around him. He had a file open on his desk and there were clippings and pictures strewn across it.

It was a file on Lexie Anderson. And it was not pretty.

One of the film assistants had furnished Cesar's office with files on everyone involved in the film. As much for security purposes as for a little general knowledge about the cast and crew. He hadn't even looked at them before now, because he hadn't been interested.

The files generally just held people's CVs. Except for Lexie's file. Her file was fat, not only with her CV, covering work which consisted mainly of TV and some indie movies before she'd shot to stardom via some vacuous-looking action movies, but also with numerous clippings from papers and magazines.

There were pictures of her, scantily clad, for a lads' magazine some years previously. One image showed her posing as some sort of half-dressed cheerleader, in nothing but thigh-high socks, knickers and a cardigan, teasingly open just enough to show off the voluptuous swells of her breasts and the sensual curve of her tiny waist. Her hair was down and tumbling sexily over her shoulders.

It was exactly the kind of image that Cesar found a complete turn-off, but right now he was having to battle with his own body to stop it responding as helplessly as if he were an over-sexed teenager all over again.

Cesar cursed and picked up the picture, throwing it aside. It fluttered to the floor. She was an actress. That was what she did.

But much worse than that were the more recent pictures and headlines: *Luscious Lexie—Homewrecker!* The tabloids had indulged in a feeding frenzy because she had been involved with a married actor who had subsequently left his heartbroken wife and children. He and Lexie weren't together now, though. According to the salacious copy, once he'd left his wife, heartless Lexie hadn't been interested any more.

Cesar knew that he couldn't have cared less what any lead actress got up to in her spare time, or with whom. But he'd kissed this woman in a moment of extreme madness only a short time before.

The imprint of that petite lush body against his was still branded into his memory. No woman had *ever* got him so hot that he'd lost control like that. He'd been moments away from backing her into a wall and thrusting up into her slick body if they hadn't been interrupted by the paparazzo when they had.

Cesar cursed. And then his phone rang. He answered it abruptly.

His solicitor's voice came down the line, 'Cesar, I've got some news you're not going to like.'

If his solicitor could have seen Cesar's expression right then he probably would have put the phone down and run. But he couldn't, so he went on, oblivious.

'You were photographed at Alexio Christakos's wedding this morning in Paris.'

'So?' Cesar offered curtly, his mind still full of lurid images of Lexie Anderson and her effect on his body.

His solicitor in Madrid sighed heavily. 'Well, it would appear that some very industrious reporter decided to do a quick search, to see if there was any connection between you and Christakos. They came up with the fact that the recently deceased Esperanza Christakos was briefly married to one Joaquin Da Silva, years before she became a renowned model.'

For a second Cesar saw only blackness. He sat down. 'How did they find this?'

'It's not a secret who your mother was, Cesar,' his solicitor pointed out carefully. 'It's just never been discovered before…the connection…'

Cesar knew this. His mother had left so long ago that no one had ever seemed to have the inclination to go digging. He came from the Da Silva dynasty and that was all people cared out.

Until now.

Cesar managed to give an instruction to his solicitor to monitor the media attention closely and put his phone down.

The press would have a field day. He was the estranged half-brother of two of the most renowned entrepreneurs in the world. It would be open season on prying into their lives. For speculating on why nobody had ever spotted the connection before now. And so on, and so on.

He was well aware that this was hardly big news—people discovered half-siblings all the time. What he wasn't prepared for was the prospect of ignominious media intrusion into an area of his life that had always been shut away. Not acknowledged.

The only time the reality of his brothers had been acknowledged, it had been used to taunt him. To drive home the fact that he was not the chosen one. That he could trust no one. Ever. As much as he hated to admit it, the scar was still deep. He only had to think back to earlier that day to remember how it had felt to be so black and bitter next to their happiness and ease with the world. A world that had taught them they could trust. That mothers didn't leave you behind.

Cesar cursed the maudlin direction of his thinking. Cursed himself again for having gone to Christakos's wedding.

With this film on his estate his privacy was already being well and truly eroded. Now this.

And then another picture of Lexie caught Cesar's eye and a headache started to throb behind his right temple. He feared that the reclusive life he'd lived for so long was about to slip out of his grasp unless he could do some serious damage limitation.

CHAPTER TWO

'MISS ANDERSON? MR Da Silva would like to see you in his office, if you could spare a few minutes?'

Lexie knew it wasn't really a question. It was an order, and she chafed at the autocracy, already imagining his dark, forbidding expression. He'd been a complete stranger to her less than a couple of hours ago, known only by his reputation and name, yet now his saturnine image was branded like a searing tattoo on her brain. *His taste...*

Hiding her reaction, Lexie just shrugged her shoulders lightly and smiled. 'Sure.'

She followed the smartly dressed young woman down a long hallway. She'd just arrived back at the *castillo* from the camera tests and was dressed in her own clothes again. Worn jeans and sneakers. A dusky pink long-sleeved cashmere top, which suddenly felt way too clingy.

The make-up artist had scrubbed her face clean and she'd left her hair down, so now she had no armour at all. She hated the impulse she had to check her reflection.

Lexie hadn't had much time yet to look around the *castillo* as she'd been busy since they'd arrived, doing rehearsals and fittings. It was massive, and very gothic. The overall impression was dark and forbidding. Oppressive. Not unlike its owner. Lexie smiled to herself but it was tight.

A stern housekeeper had shown her to her room when

she'd arrived: dressed in black, hair pulled back in a tight, unforgiving bun. She might have stepped straight out of an oil masterpiece depicting the Spanish Inquisition era.

Lexie's bedroom was part of an opulent suite of rooms complete with an elaborate four-poster bed. Reds and golds. Antique furniture. A chaise longue. While it wasn't her style, she had to admit that it was helping her get into character for the film. She was playing a courtesan from the nineteenth century, who was torn between leaving her profession for her illegitimate son and a villainous lover who didn't want to let her go.

It was a dark, tragic tale, and the director was acclaimed. This film was very important to her—and not just for professional and economic reasons. One scene in particular had compelled Lexie to say yes, as she had known it would be her own personal catharsis to act it out. But she didn't want to think of that now.

After a series of soulless but financially beneficial action movies, this was Lexie's first chance to remind people that she could actually act. And hopefully move away from that hideous *Luscious Lexie* image the tabloids had branded her with. Not entirely unjustly, she hated to admit.

The young woman stopped outside a massive door and knocked. Lexie's mind emptied. Her heart went *thump* and her throat felt dry.

She heard the deep and curt *'Sí?'* And then the woman was opening the door. Lexie felt as if she was nine again, being hauled up in front of the head nun at her school for some transgression.

But then Cesar Da Silva was standing in the doorway, filling it. The woman melted away. He'd changed. Washed. Lexie could smell his scent—that distinctive woodsy smell. But without the earthy musk of earlier. It was no less heady, though.

Wearing a white shirt and dark trousers should have

made him appear more urbane. It didn't. The material of his shirt was fine enough to see the darkness of his skin underneath. He stood back and held out an arm, stretching his shirt across his chest. Lexie saw defined hard muscles. Heat flooded between her legs.

'Come in.'

Lexie straightened her spine and walked past him into a massive office.

She was momentarily distracted by its sheer grandeur as he closed the door behind them. It was shaped like an oval, with a parquet floor, and it had an ante-room that looked like a library, with floor-to-ceiling shelves of books upon books.

Something very private and poignant gripped her inside.

'Please, take a seat.'

Da Silva had moved behind his desk, hands resting lightly on top, but not disguising his obvious tension. The desk was huge, awe-inspiring. A very serious affair, holding all sorts of computers and machines and phones.

And yet less than two hours ago she and this man had mutually combusted and she had been oblivious to who he was.

Feeling uncharacteristically awkward, she started, 'Look, Mr Da Silva—'

'I think we've gone beyond that, don't you?' His face was mirthless and hard.

Lexie wondered for a crazy moment what he would look like if he smiled. Genuinely smiled.

She burned inwardly at that rogue little thought, and in rejection of his autocratic tone. 'I...well, yes.'

Her big slouchy handbag was slung over her shoulder. She let it slip down now, and held it in front of her like a shield. Something was telling her this wouldn't be a quick meeting.

A bright colour caught her eye then, and she glanced

down to see a photo of herself on the ground. Frowning, she bent to pick it up. When she registered the image, her insides roiled. She'd been twenty-one. Completely naive. Cringing inside with embarrassment. Not that you'd know it from the picture. She'd been hiding behind a well-developed wall of confidence and nonchalance that hadn't come easily.

She held the picture between thumb and forefinger and looked at Cesar across the desk. He was totally unrepentant. Something hard settled into her gut. The awareness she had of his sheer masculine physicality made her feel like a fool. And very vulnerable—which she did not welcome. It had been a long time since she'd allowed anyone to make her feel that way.

Then she saw the open file and all the other cuttings and clippings and pictures. She didn't have to read the lurid headlines to know what the characters said even from here, upside down. *Luscious Lexie.*

She went icy. Her bag slipped to the floor unnoticed.

'What is this?'

'This,' Cesar da Silva offered tautly, 'is your life, I believe.'

Lexie looked at Cesar and right at that moment despised him. She'd barely exchanged more than twenty sentences with the man, and he'd displayed not an ounce of charm, yet she'd blithely allowed him to be more intimate with her than any other man had ever been.

Her conscience mocked her. That wasn't technically true, of course. But the other experience in her life hadn't been consensually intimate. It had been a horrifically brutal parody of intimacy.

Lexie forced her mind away from that and raged inwardly at the injustice of his evident blind belief in the lies spread before him. She hated that a part of her wanted to curl up and cringe at how all this *evidence* was laid out so starkly across his desk. Ugly.

She forced her voice to be light, to hide the raging tumult. 'And do you believe everything you read in the papers, Mr Da Silva?'

He gritted out, 'Call me Cesar.'

Lexie smiled prettily, hiding her ire, 'Well, when you ask so nicely...*Cesar.*'

'I don't care enough to give the time to believe or disbelieve. I couldn't really care less about your tawdry sex life with married men.'

Lexie saw red. She literally saw a flash of red. She forced air into her lungs. Clenching her jaw so tight it hurt, she bit out, 'Well, then, perhaps you'd be so kind as to let me know what you want to discuss so that I can get on with my *tawdry* life.'

Cesar had to force back the urge to smile for a second. She'd surprised him. Standing up to him so fiercely. Like a tiny virago. Or a pocket Venus.

It took an immense physical effort not to let his gaze drop and linger on the swell of her breasts under the clinging soft material of her top. Or to investigate just how snugly those worn jeans fitted her bottom.

When she'd walked in he'd taken in the slim, shapely legs. The very feminine swell of her hips. She was the perfect hourglass, all wrapped up in a petite, intoxicating package. Her hair was loose and wavy over her shoulders. Bright against the dark wood of his office. *Against the darkness of the castillo.* Something lanced him in a place that was buried, deep and secret. He didn't welcome it.

He didn't like that he'd also noticed her beauty spot was gone. The artifice of make-up. It mocked him for believing himself to have been in some sort of a dream earlier.

For thinking she was some sort of goddess siren straight out of a Greek myth.

But she was no less alluring now in modern clothes than she had been in a corset and petticoats. In fact, now that Cesar knew the flesh her clothes concealed, it was almost worse.

And he'd just been ruder to this woman than he'd ever been to another in his life.

He could actually be urbane. Charming. But as soon as he'd laid eyes on her again he'd felt animalistic. Feral. Even now his blood thundered, roared. For her. And she wasn't even remotely his type.

He ran a hand through his hair impatiently. His conscience demanded of him that he say, 'Look, maybe we can start again. Take a seat.'

Lexie oozed tension and quivering insult. And he couldn't blame her. Even if her less than pristine life *was* spread all over his desk.

'I'm fine standing, thank you. And where, might I ask, did you get your hands on what appears to be a veritable scrapbook of my finest moments?'

Her voice could have cut through steel it was so icy. Cesar almost winced.

'Someone working on the film compiled information on the cast and crew.' His eye caught another lurid shot of Lexie pouting over the bonnet of a car. His body tightened. He willed himself to cling on to some control. 'It would appear that person was a little over-zealous with the back catalogue of your work.'

Lexie flushed, her cheeks filling with dark colour, and Cesar felt his conscience twinge again. As if *he* was in the wrong. When this woman was standing there with her chin tilted up, defiant in the face of her less than stellar reputation.

She came forward and Cesar's gaze couldn't help but

drop to where her breasts swayed gently under her top. She stopped at the other side of the desk and put her hands on it and glared at him, her huge blue eyes sending out daggers of ice.

She plucked out the image of her on the car and held it up accusingly. '*This* is not a back catalogue of work. *This* is a naive young girl, trying to get on in a ruthless cut-throat business—a girl who didn't have the confidence or economic security to say no to bullying agents and photographers.'

She spat out the words.

'You might consider that the next time you find it so easy to judge someone you were only too happy to kiss without even knowing who she was.'

Before Cesar could respond to her spiky defence, not liking the rush of a very alien emotion within him, she'd gathered up all the cuttings and pictures, her CV and headshots, and marched over to a nearby bin, dumping the lot.

She turned around, her hair shimmering as it moved over her shoulder. She crossed her arms. 'Now, what was it you wanted to discuss?'

Lexie hated that her body was humming with awareness for this man. Who was blissfully immune to the angry emotions he was arousing.

What a judgmental, supercilious, arrogant, small-minded—

'I owe you an apology,' he said tightly.

Lexie blinked. The anger inside her suffered a body-blow. 'Yes, you do.'

His mouth was a grim line. 'I had no right to judge you on the basis of those pictures.'

'No, you didn't,' Lexie snapped, but then she flushed again when she thought of another similar shoot she'd done relatively recently—albeit for a much more up-market publication and with a world-famous photographer. But still, she couldn't exactly claim the moral high ground either... 'It's fine,' she dismissed airily, 'let's forget about it.'

He sighed heavily then, and opened up the laptop that was on the desk in front of him. 'You should see this.'

Trepidation skittered over her skin. Warily Lexie walked around the desk until she could see the laptop, acutely conscious of her proximity to him. When she saw the images, though, her belly swooped alarmingly.

It was her, and him, locked in a clinch that looked positively X-rated. Both his hands were under her skirt, pulling it up, baring her legs. Her breasts seemed about to explode from her corset, crushed against his chest. Their mouths were locked together in a passionate kiss, their eyes closed. Lexie's hands gripped his shirt so tightly that her knuckles were white. And just like that it all came back in a rush: the desperation, the craving, the *aching*. The need.

Lexie could feel heat from behind her. She swallowed. There could be no mistaking that whatever had happened between them had consumed them both. It was not a comfort.

'Where is this?' she asked hoarsely, unable to stop looking away from the image with some kind of sick fascination.

'It's on a well-known internet gossip website. It's only a matter of time before it hits the papers.'

Lexie backed away from the laptop as if it might explode...retreating around the desk, feeling marginally safer once something solid was between them.

Cesar's eyes were glittering. His disdain was palpable. He might have just apologised, and surprised her by doing so, but there was no mistaking his disapproval of the entire situation.

Stung, Lexie said defensively, 'There were two of us there.'

He was grim. 'I'm aware of that, believe me.'

'So…' She swallowed painfully, thinking of the inevitable re-igniting of press interest and the weariness and fear of exposure that would provoke. 'What now?'

Cesar looked at her for a long moment and crossed his arms. 'We contain it.'

Lexie frowned. 'What do you mean…contain it?'

'We don't give it air to breathe. You're here in the *castillo* for the next four weeks. There should be no reason why it won't die a death if they have nothing to work with.'

Something icy touched Lexie's spine. 'What are you talking about exactly?'

A muscle pulsed in Cesar's jaw. 'What I'm talking about is that you don't leave this estate.'

Fire doused the ice. Lexie pointed at herself. '*I* don't leave the estate? What about you?'

Cesar shrugged minutely, arrogant. 'Well, of course I will have to leave. I have business to attend to.'

Lexie emitted a laugh that sounded far too close to panic for her liking. 'After a passionate embrace is plastered all over the world's press, you appear in public with me nowhere to be seen…do you know how that'll look?' She answered herself before he could. 'It'll look as if you're rejecting me and the press will be all over it like a rash.'

Cesar's jaw pulsed again. Clearly he was not used to having anyone question his motives. 'You will be protected in here from the press.'

'Oh, really?' asked Lexie. 'That paparazzo managed to get in, and I assume even a reclusive fossil like you has heard of camera phones?'

She was so angry right then at Cesar's preposterous plan that she barely noticed that he'd moved around the desk, or that his eyes flashed dangerously at her childish insult.

'What's to stop some enterprising crew member from snapping pictures of *poor jilted Lexie* on the set of her new film…?' Lexie was on a roll now, pacing back and forth. 'The press will love documenting *your* exploits while I'm the rejected fool, locked in the castle.'

Lexie stopped and rounded on Cesar, who was at the other side of the desk now and far too close and tall and dark. She took a step back.

She shook her head. 'No way. I'm not going to be incarcerated in this grim fortress just to make life easier for *you*. I'd planned to visit Lisbon, Salamanca…*Madrid!*' That last came out with more than a little desperation.

Lexie had dark memories of being all but locked up once before, and it wasn't going to happen again in her lifetime—not even on an estate as palatial as this one.

Cesar looked at Lexie and was momentarily distracted by her sheer vibrancy and beauty. Her cheeks were pink with indignation, her eyes huge and glittering. Her chest was heaving. As she'd paced back and forth energy had crackled around her like electricity.

Her words hit him then: *I'm not going to be incarcerated in this grim fortress…* He felt like cracking a bleak smile. He knew only too well what that was like. And he could sympathise with her rejection of the idea.

He rested back against his desk and crossed his arms, because right now they itched to reach out and grab her and pull her into him. So close to her like this he could smell her scent, all but feel those provocative curves pressed against him.

His body tightened, blood rushed south. He cursed silently.

'So…what would be *your* suggestion, then?'

Lexie blinked. Cesar marvelled that her every thought was mirrored on that expressive face and in those huge eyes. He'd never seen anything like it. He was used to women putting on a front, trying hard to be mysterious.

She bit her lip and that was even worse. *He* wanted to bite that lip.

She looked at him. 'We go public.'

Cesar's eyes snapped up from her mouth to her eyes. His crossed arms dropped. 'We go *what*?'

'We go public,' she repeated.

'As in...?'

Her eyes flashed brilliant blue, like fire. 'As in we are seen together. As in we go out in public. As in we let people think that we are having an affair.'

Cesar tensed for the inevitable rush of rejection at that proposition. He didn't *do* high publicity—especially not with women like Lexie, whose second home was among the tabloids. Whose life was laid out in a series of lurid pictures amid salacious headlines.

But it didn't come. The rejection. What did come was an intense spiking of anticipation in his already hot blood. His brain clicked and whirred at the thought of this audacious plan. The news of his half-brothers would be hitting the newsstands possibly as soon as tomorrow...

'Well?'

Lexie's voice cut through the snarl of thoughts in Cesar's head. Somehow, without analysing it fully right now, he knew that a news story featuring *them* would inevitably be more colourful and interesting than one about his family connections. That would be diminished in favour of a far more scandalous story: *Reclusive billionaire beds homewrecking Luscious Lexie.*

'I think,' Cesar said slowly, letting his eyes fill with Lexie again, 'that your idea has some merit.'

Some of the tension left her shoulders even as she crossed her arms, which pushed the swells of her breasts up. *Dios*, Cesar cursed again silently. Suddenly all rational thoughts of distracting the press via a story about him and Lexie fled, to be replaced with the very *real* urge to touch the woman in front of him.

'Good,' she said now. 'Because I really do think that's the best solution. And the fairest.' Her mouth firmed. 'I know the press, and sometimes you have to play them at their own game rather than fight them.'

She lifted her chin then, and something about the move was so endearingly spiky that Cesar had to stop himself from reaching out to trail his fingers across her jaw. Out of nowhere came a surge of something that felt almost like *protectiveness*.

His hands curled around the edge of his desk beside his hips. He forced his mind back to the conversation. 'I have a charity auction to attend in Salamanca next weekend. We can go to that.' The devil inside him compelled him to continue. 'And we'll have to be convincing, Lexie.'

Those big blue eyes narrowed. 'Convincing?'

Cesar smiled, the anticipation inside him tightening now. 'Convincing...as lovers.'

Lexie's arms tightened, pushing those firm swells up even more. 'Oh...well, yes. I mean, that's obvious...but that'll be easy enough... I mean...I'm an actress after all.'

Suddenly the confident woman of only a few moments ago was not at all sure of herself. Cesar was more intrigued than he liked to admit. He shifted on the desk, crossing one ankle over the other, and noted how Lexie's eyes dropped to his mid-section for a second before skittering away again.

But then the suggestion that she'd have to *act* with Cesar hit home and made something hot and dark pierce him inside. He tensed. 'So what happened earlier, Lexie? Were you just practising your *acting* skills on the nearest stable hand you could find?'

She looked at him. 'No. It wasn't like that.'

Cesar felt more exposed than he liked to. 'So what *was* it like?'

For a second he fancied that the turmoil he could see in those blue depths mirrored the part of him that still couldn't make sense of what had happened. But the very suggestion that it had been in any way within *her* control and not his made something snap inside him.

He straightened up and did what his hands had been itching to do ever since she'd walked into his study. He reached for her and pulled her into him, and something treacherous in his mind quietened as soon as those soft curves fell against him.

Her hands were pressed against his chest and a soft *oof* escaped her mouth: a sigh of shock. She looked up. 'What are you doing?'

Cesar's body was already hardening against hers. An automatic and helpless reaction to her proximity and touch. He hated this feeling of being out of control—it had been a long day of that very unwelcome sensation. He gritted out, 'I'm seeing how good you are at improvisation.'

And then he bent his head to hers, and her mouth was as firm and yet as soft as he remembered, and those lush contours sent his brain into a tailspin all over again.

Lexie was drowning. Her hands looked for purchase anywhere she could find it to try and cling on. Cesar's mouth was searing and hot. Hard. His arms were welded tight around her. She was off-balance and plastered against him, breasts crushed against rock-hard contours. One of his hands moved up to her head, angling it. Their mouths were open, tongues touching and tasting. Stroking, sucking.

Lexie wanted to wrap her arms around his neck and rub herself up and down his hard length, seeking to assuage the stinging in her nipples and the ache growing inside her.

She could feel a hard ridge against her belly and it caused a spasm of damp desire between her legs.

And then the haze lifted ever so slightly, when he took his mouth away for a moment and she remembered his grim look and what he'd said, *'I'm seeing how good you are at improvisation.'*

As if a cold bucket of water had been thrown over her Lexie jerked backwards, almost stumbling in an effort to right herself. She was shaky all over, breathing heavily. Cesar was resting on the edge of the desk, barely a hair out of place, even if his cheeks were flushed and eyes were glittering brightly.

Lexie wasn't ready for this onslaught of physical sensations and feelings. Barely able to get her head around articulating much, she asked, a little redundantly, 'What was that in aid of?'

'Proving that it will be no hardship to *act* out being lovers. In fact it's almost inevitable that we will *become* lovers.'

Lexie rebelled at that arrogant tone even as her body betrayed her spectacularly. 'Don't flatter yourself, Mr Da Silva.'

He smiled. 'It's Cesar, please.'

Lexie felt dizzy at how quickly this man was dismantling the bricks and mortar that had protected her for years. She couldn't analyse it now, but she knew that he must have connected with her on some very deep level for her to have allowed him to kiss her—not once, but twice. Without even putting up a fight.

Panic galvanised her and she reached down and picked up her bag, slung it over her shoulder. She forced herself to look at Cesar but it was hard. The air between them was saturated with electricity and tension and something else far more disturbing and new to Lexie: *Desire*.

She hated to admit that she was also stung to think

that he believed she was the kind of person who would just widen her eyes and say yes to such an autocratic announcement.

She bit out, 'I am *not* an easy lay, Cesar. Evidently you believe what you read in the papers, but I can assure you that I am perfectly capable of controlling myself. I am interested in putting forward a united front in order to get the press off our backs...that is all.'

Cesar stared at her for a long moment and then shrugged. He folded his arms across that wide chest, making the muscles of his arms bunch against the silk of his shirt.

'We'll see,' he said carelessly. As if he truly didn't care if she tumbled into his bed one way or the other. As if he knew that she would be helpless to resist him when the time came.

Curbing the urge to take her bag and swing it at his head, Lexie backed away to the door, her blood boiling—and not just from his words and that arrogance. She turned around and was reaching for the doorknob, relishing the prospect of removing herself from his orbit, when he called her name softly.

With the utmost reluctance Lexie gritted her jaw and turned around, keeping her hand on the door. He was still sitting there, eyes hooded, watching her.

'Don't forget...next weekend...Salamanca. That's if you still want us to proceed with *your* suggestion.'

For a second Lexie contemplated the alternative and saw herself pacing up and down the dark *castillo* corridors or in the grounds. Trapped. With the press digging her life up again. Speculating. She went cold at that prospect. There was no choice.

She managed to say icily, 'I won't forget.' And then she pulled the door open and left, with her dignity feeling badly battered.

CHAPTER THREE

WHEN LEXIE GOT to her room she paced. Full of pent-up energy. Hot and then cold at the same time when she reconsidered the equally disturbing prospects of appearing in public *with* Cesar and *not*. And the ramifications of the press's interest in her if that was the case.

There was no doubt about it: appearing with Cesar would be the better scenario. It was only in the last few weeks that the tabloids' interest in *'Luscious Lexie the homewrecker'* had let up. If she was going to become press fodder again so soon, then she would *not* be the victim.

Cesar was unmarried. A bachelor. An affair with him would be old news very fast. And, she realised with some cynicism, it couldn't hurt the film to be linked to this kind of publicity.

What she hadn't counted on was the attraction she felt for Cesar. She'd just kissed him back again, as passionately as she had earlier, with no qualms. No hesitation! It was as if as soon as he touched her some ever-vigilant switch in her brain turned to *off* and she became mute. Acquiescent.

She held out her hands and noted that even now they were trembling slightly. Disgusted, she shoved them under her arms and then spied her electronic tablet. She marched over and opened it up.

She hated herself for it, but she found herself searching for Cesar Da Silva Girlfriend. Predictably not much came up except a few photos of him at events with beautiful women. They were all tall, brunette. Sleek. Classy. One was a UN diplomat. The next an attaché to a world leader. Another was a human rights lawyer.

There were also pictures of Cesar with world leaders at economic summits.

Lexie put a hand to her mouth to stem a slight surge of hysteria. She was seriously out of her depth with this man, and she didn't like her feeling of insecurity when she was faced with the evidence of his previous lovers' undoubted intellectual accomplishments. The plan for them to appear as lovers mocked her now. Who would ever believe he'd choose *her*?

Feeling like a stalker, she looked up his background. To her surprise, a new news article popped up. And a picture of him from earlier that very day, taken at a wedding in Paris. Lexie frowned for a second, wondering how he could have come from Paris back to the *castillo* in such a short space of time—and then she recalled hearing a helicopter earlier. Of course—to a man like Cesar Da Silva travel between European bases was far removed from most people's more tedious, lengthy experiences.

She focused on the short piece again. It had been the wedding of Alexio Christakos and his very pretty bride— someone called Sidonie. The article seemed to be implying that a familial relationship existed between Alexio Christakos and Cesar Da Silva. And also another man: Rafaele Falcone.

Lexie frowned. She knew Christakos and Falcone were half-brothers. They'd been notoriously eligible bachelors before settling down. So...what? Cesar was related to these men? Lexie kept searching and found a very brief reference to his father. Joaquin Da Silva had been famously disinherited from his family after leaving to train as a bullfighter.

He'd achieved some fame early on, before dying tragically in a goring by a bull.

There wasn't much else apart from Cesar's current accomplishments, of which there seemed to be many. He was listed as one of the world's leading philanthropists.

The picture of Cesar at the wedding caught her eye again. She looked more closely. There was a definite resemblance between the two men. And Rafaele Falcone. She couldn't be sure, but it looked as if they all shared varying shades of green eyes. Unusual. *Too* unusual.

A suspicion slid into place inside Lexie. He'd agreed so quickly to appearing in public with her, when all the evidence pointed to a man who would find that kind of exposure anathema. *He wants me.* Lexie shivered at the thought. Was he prepared to court the press's attention just to get her into bed? That idea was both intoxicating and terrifying.

But perhaps Cesar had his own reasons for wanting to divert the press? If something was about to break about his family? She didn't like it, but a feeling of empathy gripped her. And curiosity…

Just then a knock sounded on her door. Lexie's heart jumped. She put the cover over her tablet's screen and went to the door, steeling herself. But when she opened it, it was Tom—the producer. An acute dart of disappointment made her want to scowl.

She forced a smile. 'Tom?'

He held up his own tablet to reveal the same picture of the kiss that Cesar had shown her just a short while before. Her insides tightened again at seeing herself in such an alien and lurid pose.

'Ah…' she said.

'Ah…' the older man echoed. 'I didn't realise you had history with Da Silva. You never mentioned anything…'

'I don't really want to discuss it, Tom, if that's all right.'

'Look,' he said quickly, mollifying her, 'I'm not complaining, Lexie—far from it. This is PR gold dust for the film. *If* you two are…together.'

Tom was obviously concerned that an affair between her and Cesar Da Silva might jeopardise filming if it wasn't all that it seemed. He could throw them off his estate at any moment if he so wished.

Lexie's jaw was tight. She imagined the press furore after they appeared in public next week. 'Yes…' she said reluctantly, as if not even wanting to give the words oxygen. 'We are…together.'

The relief that crossed the producer's face was almost comical. 'Okay, that's good. I mean, like I said, it's gold dust for the film. We could never have generated this much press just by—'

'Tom?' Lexie cut him off, forcing another smile. 'I'd appreciate an early night. I've a lot of prep to do this weekend before we start shooting on Monday.'

He backed away, putting a hand up. 'Of course. I'll leave you to it. Night, Lexie.'

When he was gone she sagged back against the door with relief. Out of the past, the words of her counsellor came back to her: *'Lexie, one day you'll meet someone and you'll feel desire. And you'll feel safe enough to explore it…and heal.'*

Lexie stifled a semi-hysterical giggle. She'd felt it today, all right, but she didn't feel safe right now. She felt in mortal danger. Especially when she thought of those distinctive green eyes and that hard-boned face…and that powerful body. That dark, brooding energy…

She felt anything but safe.

She thought again of Cesar's nonchalant assertion that they would become lovers. A dart of anger gripped her insides. He was obviously used to women falling at his feet if he could make such a declaration. He had no idea of the scars that scored her insides like tattoos. Not visible to the naked eye, but she felt them every day. Scars she'd fought hard to overcome so she could function and live and work.

She resented Cesar Da Silva right then for inserting himself so solidly and irrevocably into her life. And yet she had no one to blame but herself.

Sighing volubly, Lexie pushed off the door and vowed to do whatever it took to focus on the most important thing in her life right now: the job she had to fulfil for the next four weeks. Her *real* acting job, as opposed to the acting she'd be doing in a week's time. Although that filled her with a lot more trepidation because she was afraid that she wouldn't have to act at all.

Midway through the following week Lexie was pacing back and forth on the set while they set up the cameras for a new shot. She was listening to the script on her mp3 player and repeating her lines to herself.

They were shooting not far from the *castillo*, in a walled garden. Inevitably, though, her thoughts deviated yet again to the person who had dominated almost every waking and sleeping moment since she'd met him, in spite of her best efforts.

He'd appeared to watch the filming at various intervals, effortlessly unsettling Lexie in the process. If he was around she became acutely self-conscious. And being dressed in cleavage-revealing nineteenth-century garb didn't help.

Right then, just as she was sighing with relief that he *hadn't* appeared today, he did appear—as if conjured up from her overheated imagination—striding towards her on the narrow path. She had nowhere to go. Trapped. All of the crew were busy working, oblivious to the seismic physical reaction inside Lexie as Cesar bore down on her in a secluded part of the garden.

Her heart sped up. She went hot all over. Pinpricks of sensation moved across her skin. Nipples tightened against her bodice. The corset became even more constrictive. She pulled the long coat she wore to keep warm more closely around her, to try and hide some of her far too buxom cleavage. She took the earphones out of her ears and fought the urge to take several steps back.

Cesar came to a stop in front of her. It didn't help that he was dressed in much the same way as when she'd seen him for the first time, in a close-fitting polo shirt and jodhpurs. Hair mussed. Jaw stubbled. He'd obviously just been riding.

For a bizarre second Lexie actually couldn't speak. His eyes were hypnotic. When *he* spoke, it jarred her out of the daze she was in.

'I've arranged for my assistant to have some clothes delivered to you from a boutique in Salamanca.'

Lexie looked at him blankly. 'Clothes?'

'For the weekend…for future events.'

Suddenly Lexie realised what he meant, and immediately chafed at the implication that he had to buy clothes for her because she wasn't as classy or elegant as his other lovers. And she hated that she'd thought that.

Stiffly she said, 'You really don't need to do that.' Lexie knew she was out of his league; she didn't need a reminder.

Cesar was obdurate. 'Well, it's too late. They've been delivered to your suite.'

Lexie opened her mouth again, but Cesar put up a hand.

'If you don't want to use them, that's fine. See what's there and decide. It's no big deal.'

No, thought Lexie churlishly, because all it had taken was a mere snap of his fingers. She looked at him suspiciously. 'How did you know what size I was?' She immediately regretted asking the question when his gaze swept up and down her body. What he could see of it…

'I asked the costume designer, just to be safe, but my own estimation wasn't far off.'

Lexie burned with indignation and something much hotter to imagine Cesar guessing her vital statistics.

Just then a PA came close and hovered. When Lexie looked at her she made a signal that she was required. Lexie looked back at Cesar and said, with evident relief, 'I have to go. They're ready to shoot again.'

But he didn't get out of the way. And Lexie knew she wasn't supposed to step onto the manicured lawn.

She was about to open her mouth when he moved closer and put a hand around the back of her bare neck, exposed because her hair was up in a complicated chignon. He bent down and pressed a fleeting but hot kiss to her mouth, and then pulled back, letting her go.

Lexie tingled all over. Her head felt fuzzy. 'What was that for?'

Cesar smiled, but it didn't reach his eyes, and Lexie felt something tug inside her, wondering again what he'd look like if he *really* smiled.

'As you so memorably pointed out, there are camera phones around. I'm just being vigilant.'

Lexie flushed to recall what she'd said to him. There was nothing remotely fossil-like about this man. He was all bristling, virile energy.

Faintly she said, 'Celeste will have to retouch my lip-stick.'

He smirked. 'Well, you'd better run along and let Celeste do that.'

For a second Lexie blinked at him. There was a tantalising glimmer of something lighter between them. But then he was turning and striding back the way he'd come, and as Lexie walked over to the main hub of the set she couldn't be unaware of several appreciative female *and* male glances that lingered in his direction and then on her with undisguised envy.

Cesar was waiting for Lexie in the main *castillo* drawing room three days later. Looking back on the last tumultuous week, he did not relish the twisting and turning of events since he'd taken one look at that woman and his brains had migrated to his pants.

Cesar was renowned for lots of things: his inestimable wealth; philanthropy; scarily incisive business acumen; a zealous desire for privacy; success. And control. Above all control over his emotions. He'd become a master of controlling them from a young age. Too young.

His usual choice of woman was tall and brunette. Elegant. Classic. Not blonde, petite and curvy, with blue eyes big enough to drown in. And with a dubious reputation splashed across the tabloids.

On some level he'd always sought to stay away from prying eyes, as if somehow they might see something in him that he couldn't articulate himself. A darkness that had clung to him for a long time. The stench of abandonment. The cruelty of neglect and a lack of care. It had been like an invisible stain on his skin.

Yet for someone who had spent his life largely on the periphery of the media glare, largely due to his very *non*-scandalous social life, the prospect of suddenly being thrust front and centre was not having the effect he might have expected.

Of course he didn't relish the idea. But at the same time it didn't fill him with repugnance.

Cesar poured himself a drink and smiled grimly. Right now though, all those concerns were receding and being replaced by something else. Some*one* else. Lexie Anderson. Cesar had been due to go to North Africa that week, to attend a meeting about aid, but had cancelled it on the flimsy pretext of wanting to make sure that the first week of filming went smoothly.

Cesar would be the first to admit that he had dismissed the film industry as flaky and narcissistic, but just one week had proved him wrong. The crew were tireless and worked twelve- and thirteen-hour days—if not longer. He was also surprised by how quickly and well they worked as a cohesive unit.

The producer had explained that most of them had worked together before, but there were lots of inexperienced locals in the mix and Cesar had witnessed more than one incident of a more experienced crew member patiently showing someone the ropes.

Lexie was one of the most tireless. Standing for long minutes on a mark while the lighting crew and cameraman worked around her. Her co-star would invariably go back to his trailer. Cesar had found out that she could have insisted they use a stand-in but had wanted to be there herself. He had to admit that he hadn't really expected her work ethic to be that strong.

She was popular. Especially with the male members of the crew. Cesar was more aware of that than he liked to admit. He'd never been jealous because of a woman before and he didn't welcome jealousy's appearance.

He heard a sound then, and with something whispering over his skin like a warning Cesar took a breath and turned around.

Bombshell. That was the only word that seemed to compute in his head when he saw the woman standing in the doorway. Her effect on him was like a bomb too—exploding out to every extremity and making his flesh surge as blood pumped south.

He took in details, as if he couldn't handle the full reality. Glossy blonde hair, trailing over one shoulder in classic screen siren waves. Pale skin. Slim bare arms. A sleeveless gold lamé dress that fell to the floor in a swirl of glamorous luxury.

She was poured into it, and the material highlighted her curves to almost indecent proportions. The deep, plunging vee of the neckline drew his eye to that abundant cleavage.

She was every inch the glittering movie star. And the most provocatively beautiful woman Cesar had ever seen in his life. He knew that if they hadn't already kissed, if he hadn't already seen her up close, he might have seen her like this and dismissed her as too garish. But right now he could no more dismiss her than recall his own name.

His hands clenched so tightly that he heard a crack, and he looked down stupidly to see his heavy Waterford crystal glass about to break in his hand.

He put it down on the sideboard with a clatter that jarred his ragged and sensitised nerve-endings.

She moved into the room, and the sinuous sway of her hips nearly undid him. Normally he had finesse. He could utter platitudes to women like *You look beautiful*. But right now all he could do was say gruffly, 'My driver is waiting outside—we should go.'

Lexie fought down a betraying quiver of insecurity as she preceded Cesar out of the room, and cursed herself for wanting his reassurance that she looked okay and not too over the top. Her dresses were normally fine—fairly standard designer fare, given to her after photo shoots or premieres—but when she'd compared them to the finery he'd ordered there had been no competition. She'd had to choose one of his.

She had not been prepared for his impact on her in a classic black tuxedo. It was obviously a bespoke suit, moulded to his powerful body in a way that most men's weren't. It should have made him appear civilised. Just like trousers and a shirt should make him look civilised. But the structured clothes only made him seem more raw. Untamed.

His hair was always on the slightly messy side, and Lexie didn't like the way that small detail already felt familiar. But his jaw was clean-shaven, and somehow it gave him a more youthful air.

He took her arm with one big hand and Lexie had to curb her response not to jump. She could feel slightly rough calluses. It made her think of how he'd looked swinging lithely from that huge horse the first time she'd seen him… muscles bunching and quivering. He was no mere soft-palmed money man. The very heart of her feminine core grew hot and damp.

She tried to pull her arm free but his hand was firm. She sent him a sharp glance, irritated at his effect on her, which quickly turned to something else when she saw him gazing at her intently. His hand slid down her arm and took her hand. It was a relatively chaste gesture, and yet it had an almost embarrassing effect on Lexie.

She let herself be led to the exclusive black car and Cesar let her go so she could slide into the back, with the driver holding the door open solicitously.

When he got in on the other side he sent her a look that made Lexie feel utterly exposed. As if he'd been toying with her, taking her hand like that.

Feeling unbearably prickly, Lexie stared out of the window. Anything to escape that dark green mocking gaze.

His voice was cool. 'This was your suggestion, you know. You don't have to look as if you're about to go to the gallows.'

Lexie tensed and felt angry. She turned back to Cesar. 'I don't regret my suggestion for a second. It's still the best option.'

The tinted windows gave the back of the car a disturbingly cocoon-like atmosphere. And since when had the privacy window gone up? Lexie's skin prickled. She could have sworn it had been down when they'd got in. And was it her or had the temperature in the back of the car just shot up by about a thousand degrees?

Cesar was lounging on the other side of the car like a pasha surveying his concubine. She almost wished he was glowering at her, as he had done that first day. She could handle that. She couldn't handle this far more ambiguous energy swirling between them.

Feeling a kind of desperation rising up, she said, 'What happened before...the kissing...it won't happen again.' *So why can't you stop thinking about what it would be like to be kissed again...and more?*

Something in Cesar's eyes flashed, but he said easily, 'We can't stand ten feet apart, Lexie. We'll have to... touch...display moments of affection. Surely it shouldn't be so hard for you to feign besotted devotion?'

That prickliness was lodging in Lexie's gut, and it made her say waspishly, 'Yes, well, I'm not the only one who has to be convincing.'

Before she could react, Cesar had reached for her hand and taken it in a firm grip. Lexie gasped as he brought it to his mouth and kissed her sensitive inner palm. It felt shockingly intimate, and a shard of pure sensation pulled at her belly and groin.

He took his mouth away, eyes glittering fiercely. 'Is that convincing enough for you?'

Lexie knew her eyes were wide, her breathing choppy. He'd just kissed her hand and she was a puddle. *Her hand!* She yanked it away before he could make a complete fool of her.

Cesar saw how Lexie shrank back and everything in him rejected that even as he saw the signs of mutual attraction: the hectic pulse at the base of her neck, flushed cheeks.

Almost accusingly she said, 'You don't look like the type of guy who relishes PDA.'

Cesar bit back the urge to clamp his hands around that tiny waist and haul her into him to show her *exactly* what he thought of PDA. Every time she moved her breasts moved with her, deepening that enticing line of cleavage. But a warning bell went off in his head. She was right, and it irked him that she'd read him so easily.

He *didn't* like public displays of affection *at all*. In fact he really wasn't a tactile person. He usually discouraged his lovers from touching him, preferring to keep their contact confined to the bedroom.

Human touch had been non-existent when he was growing up in the *castillo*. When it had come it had been rough, perfunctory. *Unloving*. A minute shove. A clip around the ear for some transgression. Worse after he'd been caught rolling around in the dirt with Juan Cortez, swinging punches at each other.

If a lover slipped her hand into his, or wound her arm through his, his first instinct was to flinch away. Except right now all he could do was see the wide chasm of distance between him and Lexie in the back of the car and resent it.

Salamanca wasn't far. And it was for *that* reason, Cesar told himself, that he said softly, 'Come closer.'

'*You* come closer,' Lexie responded spikily.

Unbidden, Cesar felt a burgeoning...lightness within him. He even felt a rare smile tip the corners of his mouth.

'I asked first.'

Lexie's expression turned mutinous and had a direct effect on Cesar's already raging blood. Arrowing directly to his groin.

'Lexie,' he growled, 'if you can't bring yourself to move

closer in the back of a car, with no one watching, how do you expect us to convince a wall of paparazzi?'

With palpable reluctance Lexie huffed a sigh and moved across the seat, still keeping a healthy few inches of space between them. Cesar was intrigued. She was spiky, confident. And yet she showed these tantalising glimpses of another side altogether...one less sure of herself.

Her faintly floral scent tickled his nostrils. He fought not to just grab her and haul her onto his lap.

'So, tell me something about yourself...'

'Like what?' Lexie's voice was almost sharp.

Even more intriguing. She was seriously unsettled.

'How did you get started as an actress?'

Lexie glanced at Cesar. The sensation that he was seeing a part of her that no one else cared to observe was acute and uncomfortable. Once again all of her deepest secrets and vulnerabilities felt very close to the surface, as if he might just peel a section of her skin back and see them all laid bare.

Right now, facing a barrage of photographers and pretending to be this man's lover would be infinitely preferable to this intimate cocoon in the back of the car. Then she remembered the awful, excoriating feeling of seeing her life spread across his desk in a series of lurid pictures and she said with faux sweetness, 'You mean you skipped the part about the casting couch in that extensive research file?'

That earned her a twitching muscle in his jaw that distracted Lexie momentarily. His jaw was so hard, so resolute. As if hewn from a lifetime of clenching it.

His voice was equally hard. Clearly he did not welcome her sarcasm. 'I'd like to know how you really got started.'

Lexie's belly dipped ominously and she looked at him suspiciously. He seemed to be genuinely interested. But that reminded her uncomfortably of how she'd once believed someone else had been *genuinely interested*. That experience had left her splashed all over the tabloids, with her reputation ground into the muck. Mocking her for how quickly she'd trusted the first person who had appeared to want to know the real her. After she'd lived a lifetime protecting herself.

The reminder was not welcome now.

In a desperate bid to avoid this, Lexie racked her brain for a pithy and superficial answer. But his gaze was too direct. Too…unforgiving.

'Well,' she started reluctantly, 'I was in a shop one day… I'd just moved to London from Ireland. I was sixteen.'

He frowned. 'You're Irish?'

She nodded, hiding the dart of pain. 'Originally, yes.' When he said nothing more, she continued. 'I was in this shop…and a young kid was in front of me. Suddenly, out of nowhere, the owner accused him of shoplifting—which he hadn't done. So I stepped in and defended him.'

Lexie shuddered slightly when she recalled the oily owner's eyes devouring her overly buxom curves. She'd developed early—another unwelcome reminder right now.

'The next thing I knew,' Lexie went on, eager not to think of that time, 'I was shouting at him. I told the kid to run…and then a woman arrived.' Lexie looked at Cesar, but he was just watching her. She felt silly. 'Look, this is a really boring story…'

'I want to hear it. Go on.'

Lexie glanced away and then looked back after a moment. His gaze was intent. She took a breath. 'The woman had heard me shouting and came to investigate. She stepped in and defused the situation. Afterwards she took me for a coffee. She told me she was a casting director and asked if I'd like to audition for a part in a short film.'

Lexie recalled how bleak those days in London had

been. How alone she'd felt. How impoverished. Vulnerable, but trying to be strong…optimistic…

'So I said yes…and I got a leading role in the film. It was shown in the fringe category at the Cannes Film Festival the following year, and it won an award.' She shrugged one slim shoulder, self-conscious all of a sudden, but determined not to let him see how easily he seemed to be able to unsettle her. 'That's it. That's how I got started. But it was a rocky road… I had an unscrupulous agent for a while… It takes time to realise who has your best interests at heart.'

For a long moment Cesar was silent, and then he said, 'I'd imagine if anyone had tried to lure you onto a casting couch you would have subjected them to the same treatment as that shop owner.'

A dart of unexpected warmth pierced Lexie—and then she thought of the lurid photo shoots she'd done and the warmth fizzled out. 'Unfortunately I wasn't always so sure of what to say no to…'

Something in the air shifted between them. Lexie couldn't look away from Cesar's gaze. It was hypnotic. He seemed a lot closer. For an awful churning moment she wondered if she had moved closer to him without even realising?

'You didn't say no when I kissed you in the stable.' His voice was deep, rough.

Breath was suddenly in very short supply to Lexie's lungs. 'Proof that my track record doesn't appear to be improving with age.'

Her brain was short-circuiting. Was it only a week since she'd first kissed this man? It felt as if aeons had passed. Cesar slid an arm around her waist, pulling her into him. She gasped, filled with a fatal but delicious hot lethargy that urged her not to think. Just to feel. He was going to kiss her, and all Lexie felt was intense anticipation. Her blood was sizzling.

His mouth touched hers. Soft, coaxing. Taking Lexie by surprise. Dismantling any feeble defences she had. His other arm pulled her in even closer and lust exploded deep in her solar plexus.

His mouth was firmer now—insisting, demanding that she respond. As the last shred of trepidation melted away Lexie's mouth opened, and Cesar's attack was brutally sensual and complete. His tongue was stroking hers, sucking it, forcing her to respond.

Without even being aware of it, Lexie touched his jaw, her fingers spreading, threading through his hair, gripping it. Learning the shape of his skull.

One of his hands cupped the weight of her breast and it sent no flares of danger into her brain. Only a desire for *more*. She arched into that hand and heard a low, feral growl of approval.

When his hand left her breast and his mouth left hers she let out a husky breath of disappointment. She opened heavy eyes to see two dark glittering pools of green and black, swirling with depths that reached inside her and tugged hard.

Cesar's fingers slid under the strap of her dress, dislodging it. Her heart-rate accelerated. The first tendrils of panic pierced the haze of heat.

'Cesar... I...'

'Shh...' he said, and that hand was busy peeling down the strap of her dress.

As if knowing just how to subdue those faint tendrils of panic, he kissed her again, pulling her under even more. Making her hot, making her *need*. Making something tight coil inside her until she had to move to try and alleviate it.

When air whistled over the bare slope of her breast Lexie tore her mouth away, breathing hard. Cesar was breathing harshly too. He was looking down, and she followed his gaze to see her breast, its nipple pink and tight and pouting. His hand seemed huge and dark against her pale skin.

'*Dios*...you are truly exquisite.'

His thumb moved back and forth over her nipple, making it pucker, grow harder. She bit her lip to stop from crying out at the exquisite feeling. The tightening sensation deep in her belly was sharper. She could feel wetness between her legs, against her panties.

She couldn't think...couldn't rationalise. She wanted to know how his mouth would feel on her. Tasting her... His tongue... But something was trying to break through. Sense, sanity...self-preservation?

Cesar pulled away from her abruptly, adjusting her dress at the same time, covering her up, and then Lexie heard it: the insistent knocking on the privacy window. A cold wind whistled over her skin.

She felt completely dazed, and could only watch as Cesar, who looked as if nothing had happened, pressed a button and said a few words in Spanish. He turned back to her, but already shame and embarrassment were clawing up inside Lexie.

An insidious image of his usual lovers inserted itself into her brain. She would bet that he didn't subject *those* cool beauties to such sensual attacks in the back of his car.

She pulled the strap of her dress up fully, covering her sensitised breast. Through the window behind Cesar's head she could see people milling, see the flashing pops of cameras. See security people waiting for them to emerge.

Realisation sank into her belly like a cold stone. Of *course* he didn't normally do this. He'd engineered that kiss purely because he'd known exactly how close to Salamanca they were. He'd known they were about to emerge from the car and had wanted to make things look as *authentic* as possible.

She couldn't meet his gaze, and tried to pull away

when his fingers caught her chin. 'What?' she spat out, livid with herself for the dart of hurt that she shouldn't be feeling. 'Do I not appear sufficiently dishevelled to make the paparazzi believe we've been making out like teenagers?'

He flushed angrily. His accent was stronger. 'That was not premeditated, Lexie. But now that you mention it...'

Eyes sparking, Cesar covered her lips with his mouth again and Lexie fought him, closing her mouth. But with expert precision and ruthless intent Cesar proceeded to show her just how pathetic her little outburst had been. Within seconds her mouth was open under his and he was bending her head back with the force of his kiss. And she was matching him, her anger heightening the tension between them.

Cesar was losing it. He knew he was losing it. But he couldn't take his mouth off Lexie's. He'd never tasted anything so sweet. Or so wicked. The way her lush mouth softened under his...the feel of that body under his hands. Her breast...that hard peak under his thumb... He'd wanted to taste it.

Dios.

Cesar finally pulled back, heart hammering. He did *not* ravish women in the back of his car. He was cool, calm, controlled.

Right now he felt anything but. He could hardly see straight. His body was on fire.

Lexie was looking at him with huge bruised eyes. She thought he'd done that on purpose. And he had—but not for the reasons she obviously suspected. He'd wanted to make sure there was no ambiguity about how he felt about her.

He cupped that delicate jaw, a little aghast that his hand shook minutely. Her mouth was pink, swollen. He couldn't help running his thumb across that pouting lower lip, feeling its fleshy softness.

'Make no mistake, Lexie, I want you...and not just to distract the crowds. You know the truth of what I said earlier. We will be lovers for real.'

CHAPTER FOUR

WE WILL BE lovers for real.

Lexie's hand was held tight in Cesar's. She hadn't had time to respond because the driver had opened the car door. And, as much as she wanted to pull free, right now she needed the support. They'd just run the gauntlet of the press outside. Lexie had felt so raw after those kisses that she'd probably looked as green as an *ingenue* at her first premiere.

Cesar had seemed as cool as a cucumber. He'd even rustled up a smile. It was galling. Shouldn't he be the one flinching and snarling?

Lexie finally managed to pull her hand free, once they were in the marble lobby of the very exclusive hotel that was hosting the event.

Cesar frowned. 'Are you all right?'

Lexie wanted to scream. She felt wild, dishevelled. Not herself. 'Not really,' she ground out. 'I need to freshen up before we go in.'

She spotted the powder room and made a beeline for it. Once inside she found it was mercifully empty and she let out a great shuddering sigh of relief. When she looked in the mirror she nearly lost the ability to breathe again.

Her hair was mussed. Cheeks bright pink, mouth swollen. Eyes huge and glittering far too brightly. Lexie pulled tissues out of the box and started to repair the damage.

Damn him. She cursed him roundly. Once again she was floored by how instantaneous his effect on her was and how her body betrayed her every time, jumping gleefully into the fire without any hesitation.

When Lexie was done she surveyed herself again and caught her own eyes in the reflection. There were shadows and secrets in their depths that only she could see. Someone like Cesar could never guess at them. She might be stronger now, but once she'd been utterly broken and had never thought she'd be whole again.

But when Cesar touched her it made her feel whole. It made her forget everything. Forget what had happened to her. There was none of the reflexive instinctive fear that had come when other men had kissed her—even if that had been in the safe environment of a film set.

We will be lovers.

Lexie couldn't seem to stem the tiny flicker of hope inside her. As inconceivable as it seemed…as unsuitable as Cesar Da Silva was…perhaps he was the one who could repair something in her that she had believed destroyed a long time ago? Just allowing that thought to enter her head made Lexie sway on her feet as a giddy mix of excitement and terror rushed up inside her.

There was a knock at the door, and then, 'Lexie, are you okay?'

Lexie's breath jammed in her throat. Her recent thoughts were too nebulous, too scary. She called out threadily, 'I'm fine. I'll be out in a second.'

When she did emerge she didn't like the spurt of emotion at seeing him leaning nonchalantly against a pillar, nor the way his gaze raked her face. He straightened up and just like that her mind started becoming fuzzy again.

She reined herself in with an effort. More people were milling around now, but to Lexie's relief he didn't take her hand again. He put it to her lower back instead, to guide her into the main ballroom where the dinner was being held. His touch burned like a brand through the back of her dress.

Lexie didn't like how aware she was of other women staring at Cesar, of the flurry of whispers that would stop as they grew close only to start up again after they'd passed. It reminded her uncomfortably of what it had been like to walk into a crowded room after the story had broken about her and Jonathan Saunders.

Cesar guided her to a seat and once she was sitting took his own, beside her. He stretched his arm out behind her, and his thumb was rubbing back and forth across the top of her bare back. Lexie almost closed her eyes as her body responded violently: nipples peaking, belly softening, warmth pooling and spreading.

His voice came close to her ear. Too close. 'Relax. You look as if you're about to shatter into pieces.'

Lexie opened her eyes and turned her head, and Cesar's face was so close she could see the darker flecks of green in his eyes. Green on green—an ocean. She had the bizarre urge to reach up and touch his face, and had to curl her hand into a fist to stop herself.

The line of his cheek was a blade, giving his features that edgy saturnine impression. Something came over her—perhaps the knowledge that she could touch him in public as it would be expected. She lifted her hand and touched his jaw. She felt it clench under her hand and looked at him. His eyes had darkened and something hard shone through their depths. Cynicism.

It made her snatch her hand back. But not before he caught it with lightning swiftness and captured it, pressing an open-mouthed kiss to the skin just as he had in the car. It was no less devastating this time.

'You are quite the actress…'

Before Lexie could respond with some acid retort that

might deflect from the fact that a scary poignancy had gripped her on seeing that cynicism, a menu was being handed to her by a waiter and she had to accept it. There was no room for poignancy; she didn't care if Cesar was cynical.

Lexie stared at the menu blankly for a moment as she regained her composure. Damn the man. *Again.*

But of course the menu still remained largely incomprehensible to her. Another kind of dismay filled her— especially when she was so keyed up. She didn't need this particular vulnerability right now.

'It helps if you turn the menu the right way up.'

His voice was low and gently mocking. Lexie's hands tightened on the thick vellum as embarrassment washed through her in waves, making her hot. She sent a glare to Cesar, who had that tantalising smile playing around his mouth again.

She turned the menu around but of course that made no difference. She could see the waiters taking orders now and started to panic. With the utmost reluctance she said to Cesar, in a low voice, 'What would you recommend?'

He glanced at her for a moment and then perused his own menu and said, 'Personally I'd recommend the quail starter—'

'Quail?' Lexie asked, feeling ill at the thought.

Cesar looked at her. 'Well, there's a brie starter too.'

'I'll have that,' Lexie said with relief.

Cesar glanced back at the menu. 'Then there's a choice of salmon risotto, beef carpaccio…'

'The beef,' Lexie said, too ashamed to look at Cesar. Especially when she thought of his multi-lingual lovers who would be well used to these situations.

He said from beside her, 'Not everyone is used to menus in French—it's nothing to be embarrassed about.'

Lexie's own mortification made her lash out. 'Don't patronise me, Cesar. I'm not stupid, I'm just—'

But before she could finish a waiter had arrived and Cesar was ordering for both of them. Lexie clamped her mouth shut. Did she *have* to let every tiny detail of her life out whenever she opened her mouth?

When the waiter moved on Cesar's attention was taken by someone sitting to his left, and Lexie was facing a table full of people looking at her with varying degrees of curiosity.

To her immediate right was an older woman who leaned into Lexie and said in an American accent, 'My dear, you've quite set the cat among the pigeons, arriving with one of the most eligible bachelors in the world.'

Lexie smiled weakly. To her relief, she discovered that the woman was as charming as she was obviously eccentric and rich, and she regaled Lexie with stories of her expat life in Spain.

Relieved to have an excuse to avoid that green-eyed scrutiny, Lexie conversed enthusiastically with the woman.

Cesar willed himself to relax for the umpteenth time. The food had been served and eaten. Lexie had managed to spend most if not all that time ignoring him. It was unprecedented. He'd never had this experience with a woman before. And certainly not with one he'd kissed.

When he'd noticed her struggling with the menu, and that she'd had it upside down, a lurch of emotion had tightened his gut. He remembered her story about how she'd got started in the industry, leaving home so young, and presumably leaving school. She hadn't gone to university. She obviously wasn't as sophisticated as the women he was used to. And yet there was something refreshing about that.

Just before they'd been interrupted she'd said angrily, *'I'm not stupid.'* But that was one thing that had never come into his mind. Lexie Anderson had more intelligence sparking out of those blue eyes than he'd ever seen in his life.

With some of his previous lovers Cesar had found himself calling things off purely because of mental exhaustion. It was as if they felt they had to prove to him what worthy candidates they were by conversing in three languages at once, about complicated political systems that he had no interest in. And in the bedroom more than one had been keen to initiate kinky scenarios that had felt anything but sexy.

But with Lexie…every time he looked at her he felt kinky. He wanted to tie her down to some flat soft surface and ravish her.

Perhaps it was due to the fact that when they'd stepped out of the car earlier, to face the press, his body had still been humming with an overload of sexual frustration, but the experience hadn't been half as painful as he'd imagined. Having Lexie by his side had seemed to mitigate his usual excoriating feeling that the lenses of the paparazzi had some kind of X-ray vision.

When he saw her dining companion get up to leave the table he felt a rush of satisfaction. Now she would have to turn back to *him*. Cesar wasn't unaware of the looks she'd been drawing all evening in that provocative dress. She outshone every other woman. Literally. Cesar couldn't even recall seeing another woman. It was as if she'd blinded him. *With lust.*

He didn't like the hot spokes of anger that lanced him every time he caught some man's gaze sliding to her abundant curves.

Lexie could sense Cesar beside her. Waiting… Mrs Carmichael had gone to the bathroom and she was ready for his gaze to be censorious for having avoided him so obviously.

Taking a breath, she turned back—and just like that a jolt of pure electricity shot through her belly. Cesar had his hand on the back of her chair again, far too close for comfort. He'd taken off his jacket and his shirt was pulled taut across his chest, doing little to hide that stunning musculature.

He spoke. 'What I said earlier...before you turned your back on me so comprehensively...'

Lexie flushed and was about to remonstrate, but she knew she couldn't. She felt like a child.

'Mrs Carmichael was interesting,' she supplied a touch defensively.

'I know Mrs Carmichael very well and she *is* interesting.' His lip curled slightly. 'About the most interesting person here.'

Lexie glanced around at the very important-looking men and women. 'But aren't these your friends?'

Cesar all but snorted, surprising Lexie.

'They pretend to be my friends because I come and bid an obscene amount of money at their auction and then go. The only reason I do it is because I believe in this particular charity and because the money goes directly to the source, rather than via a dozen government agencies.'

'Oh,' Lexie answered, a little taken aback at Cesar's words.

She'd have put him in the same category as many rich people who contributed to charity for far too cynical reasons. But this *was* a worthy charity; it was aimed at combatting sex trafficking—a cause close to Lexie's own heart. She knew it was not one that was especially 'trendy' in the media, so the fact that Cesar was endorsing it had to help.

'Mrs Carmichael told me about it.'

Cesar picked up a card with his free hand and held it out to her. 'Here's a list of items to be auctioned—see if anything takes your fancy.'

His insouciance and his air of almost bored expectation that she would expect to be indulged made Lexie feel bizarrely disappointed. Then the fact that she couldn't *read* the card sent a spurt of anger up her spine. Something bitter gripped her.

She whispered angrily, 'I might not be as intellectual as your usual lovers, Cesar, but you really don't have to treat me like some kind of bimbo just because I'm blonde and—'

'That's enough.' Cesar straightened up, his hand tensing across the back of her chair, his fingers touching her neck in a very light but subtle admonishment.

She tensed against her inevitable reaction and could have laughed. To all the world they must look besotted. Close together, staring at each other, intent...

She could see in his face that he was surprised at her response. She moved, dislodging his hand slightly. 'I'm sorry. I overreacted.'

Cesar grimaced faintly. 'I didn't mean for it to sound so dismissive or flippant.'

Lexie was once again taken aback by his ability to apologise. Slightly mollified, she said, 'Maybe I'll want to bid on something myself?'

To give Cesar his due, he didn't laugh before he said, 'Do you know how much the cheapest item is marked at?'

Lexie shook her head. He glanced down and then looked back up, naming a price. She paled and said faintly, 'I guess I won't be bidding, then.'

Cesar handed her the card and Lexie took it. She should really tell him—especially if he was going to have her so on edge—that even reading a menu would be a challenge for her.

'About the menu earlier...I should explain—'

'No.' He shook his head. 'I didn't mean to imply for a second that you're stupid.'

Now Lexie shook her head, regretting her defensive response. 'The reason I wasn't reading the menu very well was because I'm severely dyslexic.'

Lexie could feel her insides contracting, as if she were waiting for a look of disdain in Cesar's eyes. She'd seen it before.

But that didn't happen. He just said, 'And…?'

Lexie blanched. 'And…I can read perfectly well, but if I'm stressed…or under pressure…it becomes nearly impossible. I just need time.'

Cesar moved closer, his fingers whispering over her skin, under her hair. Lexie repressed a shiver of sensation.

'And are you?' he asked. 'Stressed? Under pressure?'

She wondered how it would be if she told him about the severe pressure and stress she felt under right now, with her body sparking and firing on levels she'd never even been aware of before.

Instead she said dryly, 'A little.'

He moved back slightly. 'You should have told me. A good friend of mine is dyslexic and he uses special software to help him. I'm sure I don't need to tell you of the renowned geniuses who had dyslexia but didn't let it hold them back.'

'Of course you don't,' Lexie said, almost feeling cross that Cesar was the one defending dyslexia and not her! 'I go to some of my local schools in London and talk to the kids about it—help them see that it won't limit them.'

He frowned, 'How do you manage with the scripts for your films?'

Lexie fiddled with her napkin self-consciously. 'I usually get an actor friend of mine to read them out. I record them, then I transfer them to my mp3 player…'

Someone sounded a gavel just then, and Lexie looked away with an effort. She was so engrossed in *him*. But people were sitting down again and she was glad of the interruption.

Not that long ago another man had duped her into thinking he was interested in her and she'd almost fallen for it. Now Cesar was coming perilously close to making her believe that *he* was interested but she knew that it was just lust. The spike of excitement in her gut was shameful, but she couldn't ignore it.

Cesar's attention had turned to the front. And then Lexie found herself distracted as with admirable nonchalance he made bids on the most expensive lots, only to get an assurance from the auctioneer that the lots he'd bought would be raffled for free at the charity for its workers.

When it was over, and Cesar had spent more money than Lexie had ever heard of, he turned to her and said brusquely, 'Are you ready to go?'

She nodded, too intimidated by what she'd seen to say a word. Lexie could see all the sycophants vying for his attention as they left, but he didn't stop for anyone, his hand on her back again.

His car and driver were waiting outside, as if psychically informed of his departure, but Lexie knew it must have been a series of frantic Chinese whispers from the staff, who had been watching his every move like a hawk.

Once they were in the back of the car, the darkness closed around them like a blanket, cutting out sounds, cutting out reality. It made Lexie exceedingly nervous and she scooted right over to her side of the car. The thought of Cesar kissing her again in this seductive gloom was far too scary to contemplate, even if the thought of his words *we will be lovers* tantalised her more than she cared to admit.

Through the tinted windows Lexie could see the lights of Salamanca glittering. It distracted her. She said on an awed breath, 'It's so beautiful…'

After a moment Lexie head Cesar say something to his driver in the front and then the car was turning around.

She looked at Cesar. 'Wait…what are you doing?'

A little gruffly he said, 'You should see the Plaza Mayor at night when it's lit up.'

After watching how generous he'd been to the charity, Lexie was mortified to think that he might feel the need to act as tour guide. 'It's fine,' she protested. 'I can come back again some evening.'

He ignored that and asked, 'Are you hungry for something sweet?'

Lexie blinked in the gloom. She hadn't had dessert. How did the man know she had a sweet tooth?

'A little…maybe…but really we don't—'

He cut her off. 'I know a place. We'll go there.'

The car parked on a street where couples strolled arm in arm. Cesar got out, and by the time Lexie had her door open he was standing waiting, holding out a hand for her to take. Muttering her thanks, she let him help her.

The early autumn air had a slight nip, and before Lexie could say anything she felt Cesar's dinner jacket being settled around her shoulders. His warmth and scent surrounded her like an intoxicating cloak.

When he took her hand Lexie had to battle the urge to pull it free again. The truth was she liked the way it felt to have her hand in his. She glanced up at Cesar and saw that his bow-tie was gone and the top button of his shirt was open. It made him appear rakish.

Lexie was attracting attention in her long gold dress. 'Do you think the photographers will be around here?'

Cesar looked down at her. 'They could be—they saw us leave.'

They rounded a corner then, and Lexie's mind blanked at the beauty before them. Salamanca's famous Plaza Mayor was lit up in golden lights. They spilled from everywhere and illuminated the huge ancient buildings. It was like the inside of a magical golden ornament. Lexie had known the old part of the city was a UNESCO heritage protected site and now she knew why. The square was huge…awe-inspiring.

Cesar led her across the airy space and she felt tiny in the midst of the baroque grandeur. When she was able to stop looking up and gaping at the beautifully ornate buildings, she saw that they'd stopped outside one of the cafés which was still open.

A small old man came rushing out, welcoming Cesar effusively and offering them a table under one of the massive arches that lined the square. They sat down. Lexie was relieved and disappointed in equal measure to get her hand back.

Cesar asked, 'What kind of dessert do you like?'

Feeling very bemused at being here with him, Lexie said, 'Anything…cakes…pastries.'

He arched a brow. 'Coffee?'

She nodded. 'Yes, please.'

Cesar said a few words to the proprietor, who looked as if he was about to burst with pride at having such an esteemed guest—clearly he knew who Cesar was.

A few people lingered over coffee, glasses of wine. Cesar's jacket swam on Lexie, but his warmth still tantalised her skin. It was incredibly seductive.

The owner bustled back out, with another young man following him. They set down coffee and a tray of different desserts. Lexie's mouth watered. When they'd left, Cesar explained what they were. There was an almond sponge cake, candied almonds, small fritters filled with cream, sweet puff pastry, small chocolate cakes…

Lexie groaned after she'd tasted some of the delicious pastry. 'If only I didn't have to worry about getting back into that corset in a couple of days.'

Cesar paused in the act of drinking his coffee and looked at her. Lexie looked back. The air between them sizzled. That moment in the back of the car earlier invaded her head like a lurid B movie.

He put his cup down. 'When I saw you for the first time I thought you were some kind of an apparition. That you weren't real.'

Lexie swallowed her dessert with difficulty. She remembered the transfixed expression on his face that day. She'd never forget it. While she hadn't thought he was an apparition, she'd felt something similar.

'I knew you were real...' she admitted. 'But I know what you mean. I wasn't meant to be there.'

Cesar grimaced. 'I was harsh on you.'

Lexie glanced down at her coffee and shrugged. 'Your privacy had been comprehensively invaded by hundreds of strangers...'

'I'd also just returned from my half-brother's wedding in Paris.'

He sounded so grim that Lexie looked up again. She recalled seeing the pictures on the internet of that wedding, the speculation.

Her curiosity piqued, she asked, 'So you *are* related, then?'

He frowned. 'Why do you ask?'

Lexie flushed, feeling like a stalker. 'I saw something on the internet when I went looking to see if there were any more pictures...of us.' It wasn't entirely untrue, she reassured herself.

Cesar's face was hard. 'Yes, it's true. He and Rafaele Falcone are my half-brothers.'

Lexie had the sense she was entering into a minefield. 'But this wasn't common knowledge?'

Cesar took a swift sip of his coffee and shook his head, putting the cup back down with a clatter. He was so tense all of a sudden that Lexie half expected him to jump up and stride away. But he didn't. Although for the first time his gaze was avoiding hers.

'We had the same mother but different fathers.'

'You didn't know them growing up?'

He shook his head and then speared her with a look that she couldn't read.

'No. I just knew of them. My mother was more interested in a life of opulence and luxury to think about cosy reunions, or to worry about the fact that she'd abandoned her eldest son.'

A multitude of questions hit Lexie. Why had his mother left him? But then that very first niggle of suspicion she'd had came back. 'Does that have anything to do with... *this*?' she asked carefully.

Cesar frowned. 'What do you mean?'

Lexie wasn't even sure herself. She only knew that she was feeling increasingly exposed on a level she didn't welcome.

'I mean, does the fact that it's come out about your brothers have anything to do with the fact that you were happy to agree for us to be seen together in public?'

His mouth tightened. 'I will admit that I saw an advantage in allowing another story to take precedence.'

Lexie had suspected that this might be a possibility. So why was a feeling of hurt blooming deep inside? A snide voice answered her—because she'd been seduced by his touch and his words into thinking his desire for her was his only motivation.

Of course someone like Cesar Da Silva would normally prefer to keep her tucked away out of sight, so that he could make it look as if that first kiss had been some crazy brief aberration. It had been his initial reaction.

Why hadn't she even questioned it properly at the time? His ready compliance? Because he'd turned her brain to mush exactly at the same time as he'd turned her insides molten.

She thought of the bathroom earlier—when she'd entertained the notion of their becoming lovers for a moment. The dizzying rush of exhilaration that had gripped her. *God*, she'd been so easily caught.

Lexie looked away from him and blindly picked up her cup again, not even noticing when some coffee sloshed over the rim to fall on her dress. Suddenly she couldn't stand it—being under his cool assessing scrutiny.

Almost knocking the small table over with her jerkiness, she stood up, any inherent ability to act deserting her. 'Would you mind if we left now? I'm quite tired…it's been a long week.'

She whirled away from the table and started to walk. Agitation was rising up from her gullet and also a kind of panic. Panic that she'd not thought more clearly that *obviously* he'd have an ulterior motive for wanting to be seen in public with her. He'd just been toying with her, while she'd been perilously close to proving how easily duped she could be—*again*.

She vaguely heard a muttered curse and some change being thrown on the table and just when she'd reached the middle of the golden square which by now was almost empty, her arm was caught in a big hand. She was spun around to face a familiar glowering expression. She welcomed it.

'What the hell was that about, Lexie?'

She wrenched her arm out of Cesar's grip, dislodging his coat from her shoulders. It fell to the ground, unnoticed by either of them. Words trembled on her lips, but if she uttered them she only risked exposing herself even more.

His lip curled. 'You find the fact that I have my own reasons to avoid the press digging into my life unpalatable?

That I was left behind like some unwanted luggage, with half-siblings who never even knew I existed?'

'What?' Lexie said, his words shocking her out of her own turmoil for a moment. 'No! Of course not... I didn't even know anything about your family.'

Cesar's mouth was tight. 'My mother hoped to get a good deal by bringing me back to the family home, but she hadn't banked on my grandparents giving her an ultimatum: just me or neither of us. So she left me behind.'

Lexie's agitation drained away. She put out a hand, 'Cesar...I had no idea.'

He stepped back. The huge magnificent square seemed to frame him in a leonine glow, making his masculinity even more impressive.

'That's what is about to hit the papers any day now. The full lurid story of Esperanza Christakos—née Falcone, née Da Silva—her rise from poverty to incalculable wealth and fame. And the gory details of the son she abandoned.'

Even as his words touched a painful nerve within Lexie she let out a tiny gasp of recognition at the name. She'd never put two and two together and realised that the world-famous beauty had been related to his brothers—*or him*.

She shook her head. 'I didn't know anything about her.'

Cesar, clearly angry at himself for letting all that spill out, said curtly, 'Well, *what*, then? If not that?'

Lexie's equilibrium was all over the place again. How could she articulate the fact that she was hurt because he evidently hadn't been motivated to appear with her in public simply out of sheer desire? When all along she'd protested vehemently at his arrogant assertion that they'd become lovers even as she'd pathetically melted whenever he touched her. And yet now that he clearly had another motivation it only highlighted her inner confusion and the tumultuous desires he evoked within her.

She searched his face for any hint of softness. But found

none. She realised then just how truly hard he was, and couldn't stop the tug of emotion at imagining a small child being left in that huge grim *castillo* without his mother.

Racking her brain for a way not to betray herself, she avoided his question and said weakly, 'We don't have to do this…if you don't want to.'

Right now even the prospect of staying in the *castillo* to avoid the press was more appealing than the thought of exposing herself like this again.

Cesar moved closer. His face wasn't so hard now. There was an explicit gleam in his eye that had a direct effect on Lexie's blood.

She spoke quickly, to hide her frayed nerves. 'Maybe this isn't such a good idea. If we stop now we can make it look like it was just a brief…fling.'

Cesar shook his head and said in that deep voice, 'We've gone too far to turn back now.'

Lexie's heart thumped hard. Her mouth dried. Treacherously, she didn't feel inclined to argue.

He said then, 'We both have our reasons for doing this, Lexie…and we're adults. This happened in the first place because we took one look at each other and couldn't keep our hands off each other.'

She thought of what he'd told her about his half-brothers. About his desire to avoid press intrusion around what was obviously a tender subject. Even though she didn't know the full story it resonated within her. She too had secrets to keep—dark ones. She found herself feeling a dangerous kinship with him. They were in this together.

He was sliding his hands and arms around her waist now, tugging her unresisting her body into his. All Lexie could feel was steel. Warmth and steel.

She put her hands on his chest. The moment felt slightly unreal. They were surrounded by the golden shimmering lights of the square.

Lexie's recent feelings of exposure and vulnerability were nowhere to be felt when Cesar's mouth touched hers. And they were certainly nowhere to be found in the almost shameless way she responded so quickly—opening her mouth, inviting him in, arching closer, demanding more.

There was a flash from nearby and it made her jerk in Cesar's arms. He pulled back, cursing. A photographer was feet away, snapping them. She felt Cesar tense but he made no move to stop the photographer, who was already walking away, checking his digital images.

Cesar turned back to Lexie and there was a distinctly satisfied gleam in his eyes. 'There goes any chance to protest that this was just a brief fling.' The satisfied gleam became something else—*hotter.* 'Whatever our reasons were, it's about *us* now. I want you. And you want me. It's that simple.'

CHAPTER FIVE

ABOUT AN HOUR later Lexie lay in bed with his words reverberating in her head. After that moment in the middle of that beautiful square Cesar had said nothing else. He'd just taken her by the hand and led her back to the car.

They'd remained in silence for the journey, as if both contemplating what lay ahead. Lexie's mind had been slightly numb, though. Too full to be able to tease out the different strands.

When they'd returned to the *castillo* the dour housekeeper had met them and told Cesar that he had some phone calls he must return. Lexie had welcomed the chance to escape, pleading tiredness, but she hadn't missed the intensity of Cesar's expression as he'd bade her goodnight. It had set a fire alight deep in her belly.

She could feel it now. As if she'd been awoken on some deep level. This hadn't happened with Jonathan Saunders, her *alleged* married lover... He'd appealed to an altogether less visceral side of her. Perhaps he'd appealed to the part of her that had finally been ready to trust again and she'd just chosen unwisely.

Suddenly that revelation made her heart beat fast. Perhaps she hadn't lost it completely. Perhaps she was still in control. This was totally different from what had happened before. There was no hint of scandal.

Cesar had not touched her innermost feelings and secrets. *He hadn't,* she told herself fiercely in the dark. He'd kissed her and she'd come alive. That was all. It was *physical*. And if anyone was long overdue their awakening it was her. She'd just got a little confused for a moment. Confused lust with feelings. Cesar was offering her a chance to explore this sexual attraction. And she realised with an almost desperate feeling that she wanted to. With *this* man.

What he'd revealed about his brothers and mother struck her again. That feeling of empathy. She knew exactly what it was like to want to avoid scrutiny of your most private self.

Cesar was a cynical being. It oozed from every part of him. Cynical and dark... She could appreciate why now. Lexie was cynical too—it had been branded onto her at an early age when she'd come face to face with the harshest side of life.

She'd prided herself on cultivating a sense of optimism over the years, but she knew that cynical shell hadn't really worn away completely. She could be as cynical as him now. More so. She had infinitely more to gain from this than he could ever realise.

And when the time came to walk away Cesar could go back to his classically coiffed intellectual lovers and Lexie would have achieved a personal emancipation she'd only ever dreamed about.

It was that simple.

'Thanks for a great day, everyone, that's a wrap.'

Lexie let out a sigh of relief. They'd finished shooting their scenes in the walled garden and would be moving further into the *castillo* estate for the rest of the week.

Cesar had been absent from the set all day, and Lexie had been glad of the space to try and get her bearings and remember that she was here to work. But her assertion to herself that she'd been glad of the space mocked her.

She hadn't seen Cesar since Saturday night, when he'd left her hot and bothered with that look. She'd felt so antsy on Sunday that she'd gone out for a long walk around the estate—and still no sign of Cesar.

After coming to the momentous personal decision that she would embark on an affair with him, she felt suddenly deflated now he'd disappeared into thin air. Without his unerring ability to distract her, and hypnotise her with his charisma and intensity, Lexie felt vulnerable.

She cursed herself for those weak feelings as she scrubbed her face clean in the empty make-up truck. It took her so long to get out of her costume that the base was usually quiet when she left. Only the wardrobe crew were still there, and the facility men who looked after the trailers. And the second assistant director, whose job it was to make sure Lexie was everywhere she needed to be and on time.

Lexie called goodnight and made her way back to the *castillo*. She didn't like the frisson of loneliness that assailed her and scowled at herself.

She was still scowling when she entered the *castillo* and ran straight into a wall. Except this wall was warm and it had hands that came around her arms, steadying her.

The singing rush of warmth and excitement made her scowl even more as she looked up into the elusive Cesar Da Silva's face. Damn him.

'I was just coming to find you.'

'Well, as you can see I'm here,' Lexie said testily, irritated at being irritated.

Cesar whistled softly. 'Bad day at the office, dear?'

His unexpected dry humour sparked something inside Lexie, but she pulled free of his hands before he could see it. She didn't want him to be flirty or endearing.

'I'm sorry,' she blurted out, avoiding his eye. 'It has been a long day.' *Liar,* her conscience mocked her.

She felt self-conscious in comfy leggings and a loose shirt. Face clean, hair pulled back into a messy knot. For all she knew he might have been wining and dining some dark beauty last night...

Cesar cut through her feverish thoughts.

'Those phone calls the other night...one of them resulted in me having to attend an urgent meeting in Paris early this morning, so I left yesterday.'

Lexie fought to repress the crazy lurch of relief. She shrugged a shoulder minutely and said airily, 'Really? I didn't notice.'

Cesar came close and tipped Lexie's jaw up so she had to look at him. She hated being small right now. If she'd been taller she could have eyeballed Cesar.

'Liar,' he said softly. 'Because I was aware of every minute I was away from this place.'

His words made air whoosh out of Lexie's lungs. An instantaneous bubble of lightness infused her blood. She couldn't help a rueful smile. 'Well, your meeting can't have been very exciting.'

Cesar shook his head. 'It was deadly dull.'

The air sizzled between them. And just like that all of Lexie's doubts and fears melted away again. His effect on her was ridiculous. But she couldn't resist.

He took his hand away. 'We hit the papers today...I thought you'd want to see.'

Lexie fought not to let him see how much he affected her. 'Of course.'

He stepped back. 'We can go to my apartment—it's more private.'

Lexie looked at him as he started to walk away. 'Your apartment?'

She walked quickly to keep up with him. He glanced at her and then took her hand, setting off a million butterflies.

'I have my own apartment here within the *castillo*.'

Curious as to what it might be like, in such a mausoleum of a castle, Lexie followed him down a warren of corridors, passing the study where she'd had that first cataclysmic conversation with him.

He stopped outside a door that had a keypad lock and entered a code. The door swung open. As he walked in and Lexie followed, her hand still in his, her jaw dropped. It was like stepping into another world.

The apartment was huge, cavernous. Like stepping into Narnia from behind the coats in the wardrobe. One side was dominated by a massive wall of windows. On the other side was a modern state-of-the-art kitchen. Steel and chrome with industrial lights.

The floor was wooden—parquet, like his office—and strewn with huge oriental rugs, softening it. One corner of the room was filled with three old battered leather couches and a low coffee table. A TV and music system. Along that wall was nothing but shelves and books—rows and rows of books.

Lexie felt that pang again. She loved books and reading, but for her it was a torturous process. Remembering how Cesar had responded to her dyslexia made her melt a little more.

'I have an office through here.'

As Lexie followed Cesar she saw another door, and glanced in as they passed to see a huge bedroom with a massive bed, sheets tangled on top. The image was incendiary and unbelievably intimate. She felt herself blushing. Would she be in that bed with him soon? Limbs entwined?

Her face was burning when he let her hand go inside the office. She was glad the lighting was dim and looked around. This was obviously a private study. Not as imposing as his other one, but somewhere he obviously spent a lot of time. Books were strewn around…papers. It was lived in. Comfortable. Messier than she would have imagined for someone who seemed so controlled.

He had some newspapers on the desk and turned one around to face her. Carefully keeping her expression neutral, she read the headline.

Hot! Hot! Hot! Luscious Lexie bags the world's most reclusive bachelor and richest man!

It was more or less what she had expected, but still a blow to her gut. She couldn't take her eyes off the pictures. One was of them arriving at the function the other night, her hand in his. She was practically welded to his body. She hadn't even realised that she'd been stuck to him like that. Her eyes were huge. Like a deer in headlights. Pathetic.

Another showed his head bending to hers. She couldn't remember what he'd said—something about going inside after another minute. But it looked as if he was whispering a sweet nothing. Her face was turned to his.

And one last one was a shot from inside the hotel; it must have been taken by a guest or a waiter on a camera phone. They were at the table, his arm around the back of her chair, heads close together.

Lexie felt horribly exposed, even though she was used to seeing her picture in the papers by now. But not like this. These showed just how enticing and fascinating she found this dark and difficult man. She was relieved that there didn't seem to be any pictures from the square. Even now those moments felt raw.

Cesar was perched on the edge of his desk, one powerful thigh in her eyeline, distracting her.

His voice sounding far too smug, he said, 'They look convincing…although you'd be more used to this sort of thing than me.'

Feeling prickly at his tone—obviously the experience

had been far more cataclysmic for her—and hating that he evidently believed in her guilt, Lexie stepped back and blurted out, 'I had nothing to do with ending up in the tabloids with that man.'

Cesar frowned. 'What do you mean?'

Lexie started to pace, agitated. Dammit, she didn't have to explain herself to this man. But…treacherously…she wanted to. Even if Cesar wasn't really interested.

She stopped pacing and faced him, crossing her arms in a classic defence pose. 'I didn't have an affair with that man.'

His eyes narrowed on her. 'So how did it come about?'

'Jonathan Saunders…' Lexie stopped for a moment. Even saying his name made her angry. 'We'd just done a small West End play together for a few weeks. I'd worked with him years before on my very first short film. He'd been nice to me at the time—kind of like a mentor. I considered us friends… During the play he made a point of hanging out with me. Making sure I got home okay. Stuff like that.'

Lexie felt queasy to think that his easy affection and hands-off attention had sneaked under her skin so that she'd believed she could trust him. And even though she hadn't really felt anything for him physically, she'd believed him to be a genuine friend. She'd been susceptible enough to consider that if he made a physical move she'd give him a chance. The thought made her skin crawl now.

'After we'd finished the play he called around one day and he was in a state, saying he needed somewhere to stay. He had some story about being chucked out of his house because he couldn't afford to pay the rent. I knew he wasn't that successful as an actor—it seemed believable. I had a spare room so I offered it to him and he moved in for about a week.'

'Did you sleep with him?'

Cesar's voice was sharp and Lexie glared at him, annoyed with herself for even bringing it up. It was only exposing her even more.

'I told you I didn't have an affair with him.'

'So what happened?'

'He left early one morning, and I only found out because there was banging on the door. I'd been asleep. I figured it was him—that he'd left something behind—he'd started rehearsals for a new play. I was half asleep, and when I opened the door the street was full of photographers.'

Lexie's face burned.

'I was dressed in night clothes...barely awake... I discovered later that Jonathan was actually married and had had a huge row with his wife because she'd found out he was having an affair and that his girlfriend was pregnant.'

Her mouth went tight.

'He'd known it was coming, because he'd been tipped off by his lover that the press suspected something, so he cultivated me. Made friends. Got me to trust him so that he could use me to be the fall guy when he wanted to protect his *real* girlfriend. He was terrified they'd track her down.'

Lexie sighed.

'His lover was the wife of a prominent Conservative cabinet minister; she wanted to avoid scandal at all costs. He figured *I* was a better prospect to throw to the ravenous press and he set me up well—living with me for a week, letting them believe we'd moved in together.'

Lexie looked at Cesar.

'I hadn't even known he was married. He'd said nothing at all about his wife. Or kids.'

'Why didn't you defend yourself once you knew the truth?'

Because she hadn't wanted to give the press any excuse to look into her background in case of what they might find.

A feeling of *déja vu* struck her. Here she was again, feeling the urge to *trust*, to believe. But if the last few minutes of rehashing the events of that unfortunate period told her anything it was that she couldn't trust. Not really. So she shrugged minutely. 'I didn't want to add fuel to the fire…attract even more attention. And I felt sorry for his wife and kids.'

She avoided his gaze. At least that was part of the truth.

There was something achingly vulnerable about Lexie as she stood in front of Cesar with her arms crossed so tight. He might have told himself before that he couldn't care less what she'd done, but right now he did care. And the fact that she hadn't slept with that guy made a tightness ease in him. Even as he wanted to find him and punch him. And that surprised him. Women didn't arouse feelings of protectiveness within him, a desire to avenge them. He shouldn't care.

A second too late Cesar saw that her eye had caught one of the other newspapers that had been delivered. A different headline: *Cesar Da Silva's long-lost family!*

Before he could stop her she'd reached out to pull the paper free. On the cover were recent photographs of all three men: Cesar, Rafaele and Alexio. And another of their beautiful mother. Shining out from all four photos was the undeniable genetic link of their green eyes.

Cesar stood up. Tense.

Lexie said slowly, 'That's where your green eyes come from. She was very beautiful, your mother.'

'Yes, she was,' Cesar said tightly, his skin prickling at having Lexie looking at the blatant evidence of his mother's lack of love for him. It made him feel raw again when he thought of the other night—how Lexie had all but run from the table in the square. When his irrational feeling had been that she'd seen the darkness in his soul and was repulsed by it.

Lexie gazed at him now and all he could see were those blue eyes. Something in him tightened when he saw the compassion in their depths, but it didn't make him want to run.

'Well,' she said a little awkwardly, dropping the paper down, 'I should go. I have an early start again tomorrow.'

When she turned to leave Cesar rejected it with every fibre of his being. 'Wait.'

He reached out and put his hands on her elbows, pulled her into him until their bodies were flush. The palms of her hands landed on his chest and his entire body thrummed with need.

His eyes roved over her face, as if learning every tiny detail.

'*Dios,'* he muttered. 'You are so beautiful.'

Lexie tried to duck her face. 'I'm not.'

'You are...' Cesar's ferocity made her look up. '...stunning. And I want you more than I've ever wanted anyone.'

Lexie felt the excitement in her blood obliterating the scary empathy that had come as soon as she'd seen the picture of Cesar and his half-brothers and mother. She'd *felt* the tension in his body.

Cesar's head dipped and his mouth found hers unerringly. She fell headlong into the flaming pit of the kiss. It burnt her up from the inside out, from the depths of her being.

This was *right*. She felt it in her bones. She trusted this, whether she liked to admit it or not. Her hands gripped his biceps in order to stay standing, and she came up on tiptoe, straining even closer.

Cesar undid her hair and she could feel it fall loose behind her shoulders. He was backing her towards something, and when she felt something solid behind her she realised dimly it must be his desk.

Still their mouths were clinging to one another, their

tongues tangling in a heady dance. Cesar lifted Lexie effortlessly until she was sitting on the desk. Instinctively
she hooked a leg around one of his and heard his growl
of approval as it brought his body into contact with hers.

The hard press of his arousal against her belly only
set off another spasm of lust deep in her body. And between her legs. This was infinitely preferable to trying to
rationalise her thoughts and feelings.

His hand was between them, unbuttoning her shirt.
Lexie felt hot. Yearned for air, a breeze. His touch. When
it fell open he pushed it off one shoulder, taking her bra
strap with it, tugging it down her arm.

She wanted only one thing: *more*. When Cesar took his
mouth from hers they were both breathing harshly. Somewhere she heard the ring of a phone—a mobile. She tensed.

He said gutturally, 'It doesn't matter.'

Lexie felt dazed, despite the intrusion of the phone. 'I
want to see you.'

Standing up straight for a moment, Cesar undid his buttons and opened his shirt. Lexie closed her eyes when the
intoxicating scent of man and musk hit her nostrils. Like
when she'd first seen him.

When she opened them again they widened. He was
magnificent. Broad and hard muscled. Dark blond hair
dusted his chest, drawing her eye down to where it bisected
the ridges of his abdomen muscles in a line and then disappeared into his pants.

And just like that Lexie became aware of being out of
her depth. Overwhelmed. She knew that if they didn't stop
now this would end in bed, and as much as she thought
she wanted that she wasn't sure if she was really ready.
And she realised a small part of her needed to know that
he would stop.

She put a hand on his chest and felt him tense. It almost
made her forget her intention.

'Wait…' Her voice felt rough, breathy. 'This is moving so fast…'

She looked up at him, wishing she could read what was in those green depths. Decipher that inscrutable expression.

Cesar stepped back and Lexie let her hand drop. It felt as if a chasm had opened between them. With a shaky hand she pulled her shirt and bra strap back up. She couldn't really think straight when Cesar was half clothed in front of her, and cringed as she realised it was only seconds ago that she'd been begging to *see* him.

Humiliation scored her insides. She was damaged. She couldn't just throw caution to the wind and do this. That was the problem.

She slid off the table, her legs unsteady. Between them she throbbed lightly. Mockingly.

Expecting Cesar to be irritated, put out, she caught her breath when she looked up at him and he smiled. Lexie nearly had to put her hands behind her to catch the desk. *Lord.* When he smiled something inside her ached because she hadn't really seen him smile before now.

He moved close again and rubbed his thumb across her bottom lip. His smile faded. 'We want each other.'

Lexie's heart thumped. Hard. 'Yes…' How could she deny it? God. She felt as gauche as a sixteen-year-old contemplating her first make-out session. But then she'd never had that experience.

'Next weekend there's a function in Madrid. You said you wanted to see the city?'

Her head felt fuzzy. Had she?

But Cesar didn't even bother to wait for her agreement, he just said, 'We'll go together. I have an apartment there so we can stay overnight.'

Lexie's heart nearly pounded out of her chest at the

thought but she managed to nod. 'It'll be good for us to be seen together. It'll be good for the press.'

'Yes,' Cesar agreed equably. 'But it's not just about that, Lexie. It's for *us*.'

When Lexie had left Cesar had to wait another few minutes for his body to cool down. He'd been ready to lift her up and carry her into his bedroom. His conscience mocked him—as if he could have held back from taking her right there on his desk.

When she'd pulled back, put her hand on his chest, everything within him had screamed with rejection. And then he'd come to his senses and realised just how close to the edge he was. So he'd welcomed a little space…sanity.

He was a civilised man, even though the last time he could remember feeling remotely civilised was over a week ago—just before he'd laid eyes on Lexie Anderson for the first time.

Cesar went to the window that looked out over a private section of the *castillo* gardens, tucking one arm under the other across his chest.

Something skated over his skin…a very old memory. A feeling. Vulnerability. He didn't like it. It harked back to a time before he'd made sure he was immune to such weaknesses.

He wanted Lexie, but she was dangerous. Because when he was near her he seemed to forget himself. His mouth tightened.

Everything in him had always urged him to trust nothing—and especially not women. After all, his mother and grandmother had taught him that lesson very well.

A memory came back, blindsiding him: his grandmother, dragging him painfully up to a first-floor window. Forcing him to sit down on the window seat. Every day, for hours on end. Before and after his lessons. Because she'd found him there one day. Watching…waiting.

'If you like it here so much then you'll do it every day. Watch, Cesar. *Watch*. See how she does not return for you. And when you tell me that you believe me we can stop playing this game.'

Cesar could remember glaring at his grandmother's thin, bitter face mulishly before she'd taken his ear painfully and pulled his face back to the window. Tears of pain had sprung into his eyes but he'd blinked them back. Loath to show her any emotion. Because even at that tender age of five he'd already known better.

And so he'd looked out of the window—fiercely—for hours on end, willing the figure of his mother to appear. Sometimes he'd thought he'd seen something, but it had only been a mirage. It had taken another full year before he'd finally told his grandmother what she wanted to hear.

His grandmother had made sure that he would see pictures of his mother enjoying her life in Paris. Becoming successful. Famous. A model. Having another son. His half-brother. Forgetting about *him*.

His mother *had* come back, with his younger brother, another year after that. The shattering pain of seeing his brother's hand in hers had been unbearable. He'd hated her—hated them both so much that he'd rejected her right back.

He'd lost his father before he'd even really known him. Then his mother had left him behind like a piece of unwanted luggage. Cesar's grandmother and grandfather had shown nothing but disdain and faint tolerance for their grandson. Their only motivation in making him heir had been their own greed and fanatical obsession with the family name.

The past finally receded from Cesar's head. He castigated himself for letting a woman, no matter how alluring, have this effect on him, for making him think about those things again. He *wanted* Lexie—pure and simple.

He was impervious to anything above and beyond sating himself with her. He would never want anything more with a woman than momentary satisfaction. And Lexie was no different.

CHAPTER SIX

TOWARDS THE END of that second week Lexie's nerves were jagged and fraying. It was almost certainly because of the constant presence of Cesar on the set. She felt his gaze on her like a physical touch sometimes.

She wasn't used to this. This excruciating build-up of sexual awareness and frustration. She hated Cesar for having done this to her, having this hold over her, while in the same breath she wished he would just stride across the set and take her in his arms and kiss her to make her head stop spinning.

But it wasn't just the physical sensations. He seemed to have snuck deeper. And she couldn't believe she was in danger of being gullible all over again even though this was infinitely different from what had happened with Jonathan Saunders.

Madrid and the weekend loomed large. The irony was not lost on Lexie—she was playing the part of a jaded sexual libertine and yet she had no idea of the reality of what that should feel like. She felt like a fraud, and gave thanks that no one seemed to have called her on it yet.

But after this weekend, a sly voice pointed out, *you'll know exactly what it feels like.*

When they finally called a wrap that day, and Lexie saw that it was Cesar waiting for her with a golf buggy to get her back to the unit base instead of one of the PAs, she snapped and said caustically, 'Don't you have a world leader to meet or something equally important to do?'

Cesar just looked incredibly sanguine and stepped out of the buggy to help her in, saying *sotto voce*, 'I'm your besotted lover, remember?'

Lexie stifled a snort and pulled the coat she wore to keep warm around her, hiding her voluptuous curves in the elaborate dress.

And then she felt churlish. She glanced at Cesar's patrician profile. He was even more gorgeous dressed down in faded jeans and a long-sleeved top. Workmanlike boots. He looked younger like this, less intimidating. Less a titan of industry.

As much as his presence on the set unnerved her, she'd come to expect it now. Two days ago she'd been waiting for the camera to be set up and had wandered behind one of the equipment trucks to find Cesar deep in conversation with one of the oldest members of the crew. A veteran who had worked on some of the biggest films ever made.

Cesar had been listening intently and asking him about his career. The effect this had had on Lexie was nothing short of pathetic. It had been akin to seeing Cesar cradle a small puppy. Inducing warmth, tenderness. *Danger.*

When they reached the base Cesar helped her from the buggy and opened the door of her trailer for her. Before she could go in, though, he caught her hand.

She looked at him warily.

'I have to go to London tomorrow morning for twenty-four hours. But I'll be back to take you to Madrid on Saturday. We'll leave after lunch.'

He let her hand go to cup the back of her neck, drawing her to him. Even though Lexie had a split second of realisation that he was going to kiss her the touch of his mouth to hers was still like an electric shock, infusing her blood with energy and heat. It was a chaste kiss, and he drew back almost as soon as it had started. But Lexie wanted more.

'Till then.' He let her go, stepped back.

Lexie's heart was beating fast. This was the moment. She could say something now—back out, not go through with it. *Stay safe*.

She opened her mouth. Cesar's green gaze was almost black. And, treacherously, she shut her mouth without saying anything. A recklessness within her was urging her to seize the moment.

Lexie saw other crew members arriving back from the set. Her dresser hurrying to help her out of her costume.

She took a breath. 'Fine, I'll be ready.'

Cesar smiled and it was distinctly predatory. 'I look forward to it. Don't miss me too much, will you?'

Lexie wanted to make a face but he was already turning to go. She really didn't like the impulse she felt to run after him and beg him to take her with him.

On Saturday Lexie was dressed casually, in a stripy long-sleeved top, a long, loose, gypsy-style skirt and soft boots. She had a weekend bag and was waiting for Cesar in the imposing reception hall of the *castillo*, trying not to think about the butterflies fluttering around in her belly at the prospect of seeing him again, or to think too much about what the weekend would bring.

So she thought of the difference between his private apartment and its soaring modern space and the rest of the *castillo*. So different. It made her wonder what it must have been like to grow up here…and why his mother had left him behind.

Something caught Lexie's eye through a doorway and she put down her bags for a moment to walk into a long formal room. It was filled with portraits and she shivered a little as she looked at them. They were all so stern and forbidding—much like the dour *castillo* housekeeper.

She walked around them and came to the most recent ones. Lexie figured they had to be of Cesar's grandparents. They appeared sterner than all the rest put together and she shivered again.

'Cold?'

Lexie jumped and put a hand to her heart, looking around to see Cesar lounging against the door frame, watching her. She took him in. He was wearing dark trousers and an open-necked shirt. He looked smart, yet casual. Gorgeous.

'You startled me.'

He straightened up and came in, hands in his pockets, which made her feel minutely safer. Her skin was hot. And an ache she'd not even been aware of noticing eased. *She'd missed him.* For one day.

Dragging her eyes away from him, she regarded the portraits again. 'Are these your grandparents?'

He stood beside her and a frisson of electricity shot straight to her groin.

He sounded grim. 'Yes, that's them.'

Lexie was curious. 'What were they like?'

He was clipped. 'Cold, cruel, snobbish. Obsessed with the family legacy.'

She looked at him and almost gasped at how hard his face had become. Stark. Pained.

'What did they do to you?'

He smiled, but it was hard. 'What *didn't* they do? My grandmother's particular favourite hobby was getting me to compile scrapbooks of newspaper cuttings featuring my mother and half-brothers, further driving home the message that they wanted nothing to do with me.'

Lexie stared at Cesar, too shocked to say anything for a moment. No wonder there was such tension in him when he mentioned his family. And yet he'd gone to that wedding... He glanced at her and she could see it in his eyes: *Not up for further discussion.* What surprised Lexie was the wave of rage she felt welling inside her at the horrific cruelty he'd endured.

'What happened to your father? Is it true that he was a bullfighter?'

Cesar looked away again and Lexie thought he would ignore her, but then he said, 'He rebelled. He wanted out and wanted nothing to do with his inheritance. So he did what he could to ensure that his family would disown him: he became a bullfighter. It was the worst insult to his parents he could think of. And they duly disinherited him.'

'Your mother...?'

Cesar kept his eyes on the portraits.

'My mother was from a small town down south, where my father went to train as a bullfighter. She was poor. He fell in love and they got married, had me.'

'Did she know who he was? Where he'd come from?'

Now Cesar looked at Lexie, and she almost took a step back at the cynicism etched on his face. He seemed older in that moment.

'Of course she did. That's why she targeted him. If he hadn't died she probably would have persuaded him to return home—especially once they'd had me.'

Lexie tried to hide her dismay at seeing this side of him. He seemed utterly unapproachable at that moment.

'You don't know that for sure, though...' she said, almost hopefully.

'Of course I know,' he dismissed coldly. 'As soon as my father died she brought me here, but my grandparents wanted nothing to do with her. Only me. They realised that their legacy would be secure with an heir. Once she knew there was nothing she could gain, she left.'

Lexie put a hand to her belly in a reflexive action as

the old pain flared inside her hearing his words. To think of the awful wrench it must have been for his mother to give him up. No matter what he said, she couldn't have been that cruel.

'But she came back…? You said that she came back some years later.'

A bleak look flashed across Cesar's face, but it was so fleeting that Lexie wasn't even sure she'd seen it.

'Yes, she did. Maybe she thought she could benefit then. But it was too late.'

'How old were you?'

'Almost seven.'

Lexie gasped. 'But that's so young…you were still so young. Why didn't you go with her?'

Even as she realised that Cesar wasn't going to answer her she had a moment of intuition. He'd been left here when he was so tiny, yet he had been old enough to remember. Remember his mother walking away. Lexie couldn't even begin to imagine what had broken inside him in those years after his mother had left him. Broken so badly that he'd let her walk away from him again.

Cesar stepped back and said, 'We should go. The plane is ready.'

After a short trip in a sleek Land Rover to a local airstrip, Lexie knew she shouldn't have been surprised to see a small private plane waiting for them—reminding her, as if she needed it, just who she was dealing with.

Except the man she was dealing with had just shown her a side of himself that was raw and bleak, and she couldn't stop her chest from aching. Even though she knew that he wouldn't thank her for it. He hadn't had to say a word for her to know that he would scorn the slightest hint of pity.

Cesar parked the car and swung out of the driver's seat

with lithe grace. He'd come around to help Lexie out before she could object, taking her hand in his firm grip.

An assistant took their bags to the plane. The pilot was waiting to greet them, and then they were stepping into the plush, luxurious world of the super-rich. Although Lexie was still a bit too shaken up by what Cesar had revealed to truly enjoy this novel experience.

A steward showed her to her seat solicitously, and Cesar took the seat opposite. There was no waiting for other people to arrive, to sit down. Once they were in they buckled up and the plane was moving.

In a bid to try and shake some of the residual melancholy she felt at hearing about Cesar's less than happy-sounding childhood, Lexie asked, 'So what's the function this evening?'

Cesar stretched out his long legs across the aisle. 'It's a dinner and Spanish music event at the Italian Ambassador's residence.'

Lexie felt her stomach plummet. 'Seriously? But I've never met an ambassador in my life…I won't know what to say—'

He leaned across and took one of her hands out of her lap and held it to his mouth, kissing it. Effectively shutting her up. The air in the cabin seemed to get hot and sultry.

'You don't have to worry about saying anything. They're not going to present you with an IQ questionnaire before dinner to see if you qualify.'

Lexie hated this insecurity that stemmed not only from her dyslexia but from having left school early. 'But they'll be talking about politics and the EU and economics…'

'And,' Cesar replied without hesitation, 'if they do I can't imagine that you wouldn't know just as much if not more than them. These are *people*, Lexie, they're not intellectual giants.'

'Well, you are…' She was being distracted by the hypnotic stroke of Cesar's thumb on the underside of her wrist. His thumb stopped and he frowned at her.

'Where on earth do you get that from?'

Lexie shrugged, feeling exposed again for having researched him in the beginning.

'You're one of the most successful men in the world… you go to economic forums…all those books in your study and apartment…'

Cesar's mouth twisted. 'All those books in my study belong to my family. The only reason I haven't ever got rid of them is in case I need them for reference and for reasons of pure vanity—because they look good.' Then he said, 'Me, though? The books I like reading are popular crime thrillers—nothing more intellectual than that, I assure you.'

Something shifted inside Lexie. An ominous feeling of tenderness welled up.

'And as for school…I was not a natural A student—far from it. I had to work for every one of my grades. Once my grandparents realised this they recruited the local swot— Juan Cortez, who is now the Mayor of Villaporto, the local town—to come and help me.'

The tenderness swelled. 'Are you still friends?'

Cesar smiled. Another rare, proper smile. Lexie had to stop herself from gripping his hand tighter.

'Yes, but only because we nearly killed each other when we were ten.'

Lexie asked impulsively, 'What happened?'

He looked rueful. 'I had issues with someone being smarter than me.' And then he said, 'I'm a hustler, Lexie. I go to these forums and meetings because I have inherited and manage a vast legacy. For a long time I thought I wanted to do what my father had done and turn my back on it, but then I realised that if I did and the fortune got carved up I'd be cutting off my nose to spite my face. I realised that I enjoyed being an entrepreneur—I was good at it. And once my grandparents died I could finally put the family's vast wealth to some good use.'

'How old were you when they died?'

Cesar's easiness vanished. 'Fifteen when my grandfather died and then eighteen when my grandmother died.'

Lexie squeezed his hand but said nothing. She could see the lack of grief for them in his eyes—it was almost defiant. Her own silly heart ached to think of him taking on all that responsibility at such a young age. And as a boy growing up with no love. The thing was, she knew what that felt like—albeit on a different level.

The lack of affection in her own family had come after shattering events and had never been repaired.

The steward appeared then, to offer them some refreshments, and Cesar let her hand go. To Lexie's relief the conversation turned to more neutral topics after that.

It felt like no time at all before they were descending into Madrid, and Lexie looked out of the window eagerly to catch her first glimpse of the capital city.

When they emerged from the plane after landing it was pleasantly warm with a hint of autumnal freshness. A car was waiting for them.

Cesar said in the back of the car, 'We'll go to the apartment and then I'm taking you out on a tour.'

'Okay,' Lexie answered. An incredibly light feeling was bubbling up inside her, and she was determined not to analyse it too carefully.

When Cesar put out his hand for her to come closer she didn't hesitate, sliding along the back seat until she was right beside him. His arm went around her, his fingers splaying provocatively just under Lexie's breast, making her toes curl in her shoes.

His apartment building was on a very grand, wide, tree-lined street. It was an old building, and his apartment was at the top. When he opened the door to let her in Lexie wasn't surprised to see that the same kind of modern design as was in his *castillo* apartment ran through this space too. The old building was the shell, but classic furniture and abstract paintings gave it a very contemporary and slightly eclectic Art Deco aesthetic. It oozed class and luxury. Good taste.

Lexie asked, as he led her down a corridor, 'Did you design this and your other apartment at the *castillo*?'

'Yes. A friend who is an architect helped me. Luc Sanchis. He oversaw the structural work and his team did the interiors.'

'Wow,' Lexie said, awed. Even she'd heard of the famous constructive architect.

Cesar stopped at a door. 'We've also come up with a plan to completely remodel the interior of the *castillo* but it's undergoing a lengthy planning permission process. As you can imagine it's protected because it's so old, and we have to incorporate that integrity with the new design.'

Lexie wrinkled her nose. 'I think it would be great… It's an amazing building, but…'

'Completely stuck in the Middle Ages and not in a good way?'

She smiled. 'If you say so. I couldn't possibly be so rude.'

He reached out and rubbed his thumb along her lower lip. Lexie's blood sizzled. And then, as if he had to make a physical effort to stop touching her, he gritted his jaw and let his hand drop.

He pushed open the door and let her precede him. It was a bedroom, with a massive en-suite bathroom and dressing room. The same Art Deco stamp on the furnishings. She loved it.

'This is your bedroom.'

She turned around, her heart speeding up. He was putting her bags at the bottom of the bed and turning around.

'I'm not even going to say it, Lexie... You know I want you. But this is your space.'

Beyond touched, and reassured in a very deep place that *needed* reassurance, Lexie got out a husky 'Thank you...'

A few hours later Cesar stood at the window in the reception room. He was waiting for Lexie, his hands stuck deep in the pockets of his black trousers. His hands had never itched so much in his life. The previous few hours had been both heaven and hell. Torture.

When he'd asked her how she'd like to see the city and she'd professed an interest in an open-top bus tour that was what they'd done.

He'd never done one of these tours in his life—it was completely alien to anything he'd normally do—but he had noticed them in various cities and always envied the kind of people who went on them.

Lexie had been like a child, her face lighting up to see the beautiful city. And Cesar had ended up inadvertently doing a better job of being tour guide than the actual tour guide. A small crowd had gathered around them on the top of the bus so they could hear his take on the various sites. It had helped that he spoke multiple languages.

Lexie had been laughing when they disembarked, because some of the American tourists had insisted on tipping him—one of the wealthiest men in the world!

In that moment, when Lexie had been laughing, Cesar had felt a dizzying rush of something that was also completely alien to him...it was only now that he could recognise it with a sort of incredulity. *Happiness.*

For a moment he'd felt pure, unadulterated ease. Joy. The blackness that seemed to be his constant companion had dissipated. And it had lasted even as Lexie had asked if they could walk back to the apartment because it wasn't far.

They'd stopped and had coffee and cakes on the way.

Cesar had never, ever spent such an enjoyable couple of hours with anyone.

The threads of that happiness lingered now, like a seductive caress. But Cesar was aware of something very strong inside him that refused to believe it. It was urging him to be vigilant, not to trust in this ephemeral feeling.

Anything that had felt vaguely like this had been ripped away from him at such an early age that now it seemed too...*easy*.

He heard a sound then, and turned around, and when he saw Lexie it was like a punch to his gut—it was that physical.

He couldn't have analysed what she was wearing in any kind of detail. All he knew was that it was black and seemed to cling to every curve she had with a precariousness that made Cesar's body stiffen in wanton reaction. Her shoulders were bare. Her hair was pulled back, revealing her long delicate neck.

She was a goddess.

Cesar walked over to her before he could melt into a pool of unrestrained lust and lock them both in this apartment until she finally gave in to him. He was actually afraid to touch her—afraid that if he did he'd turn into some feral being.

'My car is waiting outside.'

Lexie smiled, but Cesar could see a slight nervousness in her eyes. The thought of dinner? Was she feeling insecure? It made unwelcome protectiveness rise up, but lust was also rising, too high and fast for him to be able to focus on it or let it bother him.

He let her precede him, her scent light and fresh. Floral. Her long dress swung around her hips and legs, and Cesar all but closed his eyes and sent a prayer up to the God he hadn't consulted in a long time for the ability to show some restraint.

* * *

Lexie was finally relaxing. Although she knew it probably had as much to do with the second glass of wine she was on as the fact that the dinner was proving to be far less scary than she'd thought.

But the location was beyond intimidating in its grandeur. It was a very old palace in the centre of Madrid that had been turned into the Ambassador's residence. If everyone hadn't been in modern clothes it would have been hard to ascertain where the past ended and the present began under the soft, seductive lighting of hundreds of candles.

She'd imagined that people would be talking about complicated fiscal policies and the merits of a single currency, but they were actually far more interested in talking to her about the famous people she'd met and what they were really like.

She felt a large hand on her thigh and her lower body spasmed in pure need. She put her hand over his to remove it, but instead her fingers wound their way through his. Holding him there. Her body and her mind were in two different places...

She smiled brightly at the man beside her and took advantage of the lull in the conversation to turn and face Cesar on her other side.

He looked at her. 'Okay?'

She smiled wryly. 'I've been telling the esteemed Secretary to the Greek Ambassador exactly which celebrity tour he should take his kids on when they go to LA next month.'

Cesar smiled and leant forward to kiss her on the mouth. Lexie found herself wanting to cling to him, her fingers tightening on his on her thigh. *She was ready.* Her heart sped up at the thought even as old tendrils of fear made her trepidatious.

He drew back and his eyes were glowing dark green.

'There's a dance showpiece after dinner. We don't have to stay if you don't want to.'

Lexie shook her head, giving in to that fear like a coward, delaying the moment of inevitability. 'No, it's fine. I'd like to see it.'

As the dinner ended and they moved into the room where the showpiece was taking place Lexie seemed to be existing in a haze of shimmering heat. She was acutely aware of Cesar's every move.

Their afternoon on the bus had been delicious torture. Cesar had been dressed down, in jeans and a casual top and jacket. He'd pressed so close against her that she had barely taken in a word he'd said about any of the stunning monuments and squares they'd seen, all too aware of him.

He'd been so gracious and patient when the other tourists had wanted to listen to his explanations and she'd seen another side of him completely. He wasn't as misanthropic as first impressions would have led Lexie to believe—far from it. But she wondered if he even realised that himself.

They had front row seats for the dance performance— by a flamenco dancer. When the lights went down a hush went around the crowd and then a lone guitar started playing the most hauntingly beautiful Spanish music.

Lexie glanced at Cesar to find him staring at her with an intensity that made her insides liquefy. Only with extreme effort could she look away.

A spotlight lit up the small stage and a beautiful dark-haired woman with the lithe body of a dancer walked into the middle. She wore a long red dress, very plain and simple, red shoes, and a red flower in her hair.

She made the most exquisite shapes with her hands and body—typical flamenco postures. Then the hard soles and heels of her shoes started hitting the boards of the stage as the rhythm of the guitar picked up pace. Tiny hairs stood up on the back of Lexie's neck.

It was mesmerising. There was something so elemental and beautiful about this woman and the power in her body. It made a ball of emotion lodge in Lexie's chest and throat. She was acutely aware of the man beside her, of his sheer overwhelming masculinity. Something seemed to be flowing between them through the beat of the music, even though their thighs and arms were barely touching. It was carnal and earthy. Sexual.

The beat and power of the dancer's feet seemed to resonate with Lexie's heartbeat. Cesar had unlocked something powerful within her—something that she was finally connecting with herself after such a long time.

The beat of her own sexuality.

It was something she'd feared lost for ever, stolen from her too long ago ever to claim it back. Lexie wanted to look at Cesar again, but she was afraid that if she did, and he was looking at her, he'd see how raw her desire for him was.

She could see the sheen of exertion on the dancer's skin. The music and the dance were building and building. Lexie fancied she must have a similar sheen to *her* skin…she felt so hot. The expression on the woman's beautiful face was intense as her feet beat out the relentless passionate rhythm. Lexie felt it rise up through her body too.

As the music and the dance reached a crescendo, and as if he could sense how affected she was, Cesar's hand closed around Lexie's, his fingers twining through hers with an unmistakably possessive touch.

Her nipples pricked painfully. She was breathing harshly, every part of her body tingling with desire for the man beside her, as the music exploded and the woman came to a dead stop with her arms high in a proud and beautiful pose, her chest heaving with exertion. People started to clap rapturously. But still Lexie was almost afraid to look at Cesar.

'Lexie?'

She finally turned her head towards him and her world coalesced down to this moment and this man. She wanted him with a fierce drumbeat of need.

Another performer was coming on and she said impulsively, 'Would you mind if we left now?'

Cesar shook his head, a frankly explicit look coming into his eyes as if he could read what was on her mind, feel her desire. 'No—let's go before the next act starts.'

By the time they were walking out Lexie had taken deep breaths and regained some control. But she still trembled all over. Never had anything impacted her in such a deeply physical and visceral way as it had sitting beside this man and wanting him so badly that their very surroundings seemed to echo with it.

They were at the front of the residence now and Cesar's car was pulling up. The driver opened the door for her and Cesar got in on the other side. He reached for her almost immediately and Lexie went willingly.

Their mouths met and their kiss was hungry and desperate. Lexie's blood thundered and roared. She was still borne aloft on the sheer exhilaration of the dance. She drowned in the kiss, in the rough stroke of Cesar's tongue against hers and the feel of his arms around her.

By the time they reached the apartment she was half sitting on his lap, arms around his neck, mouth swollen, breathing fast.

Gently he took her arms down and opened his door before stepping out. He reached in and Lexie had one crazy moment of thinking she could just shut the door, instruct the driver to drive all the way back to the *castillo* and shut out the clamours of her body.

But she didn't. She'd already proved to herself that she was strong enough to withstand the worst things that could happen to a woman. She was certainly strong enough to withstand reclaiming her body and her right to sensual pleasure.

Lexie put her hand in Cesar's and let him pull her out. Keeping a tight grip on her hand, as if he was aware that a rogue part of her still wanted to escape, he greeted the concierge and led her to the lift. Once inside they didn't speak. But the air hummed with awareness and expectation. It was heavy.

When they entered his apartment and the door closed behind them the silence swirled around them. Lexie's heart was beating so hard she thought it had to be audible.

Cesar shrugged off his jacket and threw it over a chair haphazardly. Looking at Lexie, he pulled at his bow tie, undoing it. She was clutching her bag tightly, her eyes glued to his mouth, wanting it on hers again.

He reached down and took her bag, threw it aside to join his jacket. Then he put his hands on her arms.

'You're sure?'

After a moment Lexie nodded and said, 'I've never been more sure of anything in my life. Make love to me, Cesar.'

CHAPTER SEVEN

FOR A MOMENT Cesar did nothing, and a wave of cold clammy horror gripped Lexie as she imagined being rejected. But then he dipped, and she let out a little squeal when he lifted her into his arms against his chest.

He strode down the corridor, past her bedroom to another door on the opposite side. Lexie took in no details of the room he walked into beyond the fact that it was dark, palatial and had a massive bed.

He walked right over to it and let Lexie down, before reaching for a light and switching it on to put out a pool of golden light.

Light, Lexie thought. *Light is good*. The enormity of what she was doing was sinking in.

Reverently Cesar put his hands on Lexie's shoulders. She tried to calm her thundering pulse. Then he turned her around and it went haywire again.

He pulled the pins from her hair until it fell down. Then he brushed it aside over one shoulder. Lexie shivered when she felt him come close behind her, wrapping an arm around her midriff and pressing a kiss to her bare shoulder.

His fingers were on her zip at the back of her dress. Slowly, so slowly, he started to pull it down. The dress loosened around her chest and she curled her hands into fists to stop herself from impeding its progress as it fell forward and down.

Now she was bare from the waist up except for a strapless lace bra.

Cesar's hand had drawn the zip all the way to the top of her buttocks, where it ended. Then with both hands he pushed it over her hips so that it fell to the floor. She was aware of a rough indrawn breath, and then his hand was cupping her bottom in her silk French knickers, smoothing over her hip.

Her legs were losing their ability to hold her upright.

When he put his hands on her shoulders again, to turn her around, Lexie looked down. She felt hot, excited and scared. All at once. Cesar's hands were on her waist, pulling her into him.

'Lexie...look at me.'

She bit her lip, but looked up. His face was flushed, eyes glittering like dark jewels. His gaze dropped to her mouth, and then lower. Her skin went on fire.

He lifted a hand and cupped one breast. Her nipples were hard and stinging. Pushing against the lace of her bra. He brushed his thumb across one nipple, making Lexie gasp. Making her want more. *His mouth.*

Cesar sank back onto the bed and pulled her into him. Lexie nearly stumbled in her shoes and she kicked them off jerkily, steadying herself on his shoulders.

His hands closed around her waist again, and with her breasts at easy reaching distance for his mouth he explored her through the lace, his tongue laving the lace-covered tips, first one and then the other.

Lexie's hands were like claws gripping his shoulders. It was torture. The stinging chafing of the lace against those throbbing moist peaks. She almost sobbed with relief when he reached around to undo her bra and then cupped one breast before he encircled that aching naked tip with his wicked, hot mouth. It was exquisite.

Her hands moved to Cesar's head, fingers threading through silky strands of hair. When he tried to draw back she had to release him. She looked down, dazed, drunk. Instinctively she reached for his shirt, undoing his buttons, her breasts swaying with her movement.

He took over, emitting a soft growl of impatience when a button got caught, ripping it apart and off. Then his chest was bare. And gorgeous. Lexie had to sink down onto one thigh, unable to stand any more.

Cesar caught her to him with a strong arm, his other hand finding her chin and angling it so that he could plunder her mouth in a scorching hot kiss. He let that hand trail down to cup and massage her breast again, fingers pinching her stiff nipple.

Lexie squirmed. Between her legs she was stinging. Moist. Sensing her need even before she acknowledged it, Cesar moved his hand down over her waist. He pushed her legs open, his mouth still on hers, distracting her, until she felt those fingers exploring the delicate skin of her inner thigh. She held her breath as they trailed over her sex, hidden under the silk of her panties.

Lexie broke the kiss. Cesar's eyes were half lidded, hot with need. She was clinging to him and his hand was *there*, right where she felt swollen and needy. He was pressing against her flesh, moving rhythmically.

In a fast-moving world that had been reduced to all things physical Lexie tried to cling onto reality and the feeling that she could trust Cesar.

She put her hand on his wrist, stopping his movements, and said threadily, 'I don't want you to hurt me.'

He could never know the wealth of history behind that plea.

He frowned and removed his hand, bringing it up to touch her jaw again.

'I would never hurt you. We'll take this slow, okay?'

Lexie nodded. Relief flooded her. In a smooth move, Cesar lifted her from his lap and onto the bed. She sank back and looked up, watching him undo his trousers and push them down.

Her eyes widened on the bulge in his boxers, and they widened even more when he'd dispensed with the rest of his clothes and put his hands to the edges of those boxers. He pushed them down and his erection was freed.

Lexie waited for rejection, revulsion, fear...but it didn't come. She only felt intense excitement. And need. Euphoria bubbled up inside her. Lightness. When Cesar bent down and put his hands to her panties she lifted her hips to let him pull them down.

His body was awe-inspiring. He was a very masculine man in his prime. Broad through the chest and shoulders, slimming to lean hips, and down to powerful buttocks and thighs.

He came down on the bed beside her, on one arm, and looked at her. His gaze left scorching hot trails where it rested on her curves. 'You're more beautiful than anything I've ever seen.' He ran his hand up and down her body, barely skimming, teasing her.

Lexie touched his jaw reverently, feeling the tough line under her fingers, following the line of his cheek down to his mouth, tracing that sensual shape.

Her belly contracted when he caught her hand and sucked one finger deep. Then he took her finger out of his mouth and, not taking his eyes off her, trailed his hand down over her breasts to the curls protecting her sex.

Gently, he encouraged her to open her legs. Lexie held her breath. Keeping the heel of his hand against her, he explored her with his finger, seeking the seam of her body and parting it, releasing her desire to smooth his passage.

She was breathing again, but it was laboured as Cesar moved his fingers over her and pressed his palm against her. Without her even knowing it Lexie's body was moving, hips twitching, circling, seeking more.

He bent his head and took her mouth, and she almost sobbed into it when she felt him thrust one finger inside her. Her hands had to hold onto something and she found his arms, fingers digging into hard muscles. Cesar shifted and she could feel his erection against her hip.

She was too shy to reach out and touch it, but she wanted to. Wanted to explore what all that power would feel like encased in silken skin.

But right now his finger was moving in and out of her body and causing sensations such as Lexie had never experienced before. There was a delicious tightening feeling, building and building. An urgency. A desire for more.

When one finger became two, and Cesar's tongue thrust deep into her mouth, her hands tightened on him.

He broke away. '*Dios*...you're so responsive...I don't know how slow I can go...you're killing me.'

Lexie blinked. Cesar looked like a dark golden lion in the dim light. She whispered throatily, 'Don't go slow.'

He gazed at her, his breath coming sharp and fast. He was on the edges of his control...she could sense it. Right then Lexie felt invincible. Strong. In control.

Cesar disappeared for a moment and Lexie heard a drawer open and shut, then the sound of foil ripping. He came back and she saw him smoothing protection onto his erection.

A spurt of jealousy that he was touching himself so intimately caught her unawares, making her want to giggle with the sheer joy of discovering her own body again. Of being here and feeling *safe*.

Cesar came over her, careful not to crush her, but the weight of his naked body over hers was something Lexie craved. She reached for his body, clasping him, urging him down.

He cursed. 'I don't want to hurt you.'

'You won't,' she said, and meant it, feeling emotional.

Lexie felt him push her legs apart further with his hips, stretching her. Poised above her, he nearly undid her when he pushed some hair back off her hot cheek and pressed a kiss to her mouth. As if somehow...he *knew*.

And then she felt him—hard, forceful, pushing into her, seeking her acceptance. Her body resisted and Lexie sucked in a breath. She willed herself not to let the darkness of her past reach out to poison this moment. She willed her body to relax, to *trust*.

After several heart-stopping moments, punctuated only by their harsh breathing, she felt a shift and Cesar's body slid in a little more. Filling her.

'You're so small...so tight.'

She moved her hips experimentally and earned herself a long, low growl from Cesar that sounded feral.

She could see the cost of his restraint showing on his face, in his tense shoulders. He reached down a hand and moved it under her thigh, encouraging her to lift her leg around his waist.

The movement brought him deeper into her body, and now Lexie groaned as excitement built, a restless, surging yearning for a deeper connection between their bodies.

She lifted her other leg and Cesar pulled out before sliding back in, his body huge and powerful. He angled his body so that he was thrusting as deep as possible. He put a hand between them and found the cluster of cells at the juncture of her thighs. Lexie gasped out loud as that building excitement shot right through her core.

Her whole body was alive with a deep mystical energy, coiling and binding her to this man with an invisible weave. Cesar's chest touched hers, hair a delicious friction against her breasts. Lexie arched her back to ask mindlessly for *more*.

Cesar's movements were becoming more urgent, stronger. Faster. Her heels were digging into his muscular buttocks, driving his body deeper into hers, holding him to her.

She could feel wave after wave of ecstasy washing through her until they gathered such force that she begged Cesar to release her from the torture and let her fly. But she wasn't coherent.

He bent his head and kissed her. 'It's okay, *querida*, I'll catch you.'

Those words unlocked the tension and Lexie soared on a blissful plateau of pleasure so intense that it was almost painful. And as she fell, feeling the powerful contractions of her body around Cesar's, she bit his shoulder to stop herself from screaming out loud. His own body tensed powerfully before he let out a guttural shout, and he fell just behind her.

Cesar's brain was in meltdown. Even now he could still feel the ripples of Lexie's orgasm keeping his body hard, not letting him come down completely from the most intense climax he'd ever experienced.

It was the most difficult thing in the world to break the connection between their bodies, but Cesar gritted his jaw and moved, releasing them both. Lexie winced minutely. Her eyes were wide, cheeks flushed, hair in disarray around her head.

He moved so that he didn't crush her and came onto his side, pulling her into him so that they were face to face. Normally when Cesar made love to a woman he felt the overwhelming need to get away. Right now it was the last thing on his mind. She fitted him. One leg was still looped over his thigh. The centre of her body was still flush with his, doing little to help his arousal subside.

He could only look at her. The expression on her face was as stunned as he felt. A lock of hair was across one hot cheek, damp with her sweat. He raised a hand, noted vaguely that it was trembling, and tucked her hair behind her ear.

As his normal faculties returned Cesar was aware of feeling more and more vulnerable. But still he couldn't seem to move, to be able to unweld his arms from around her.

Then he saw a brightness in her gaze in the dim light. Her mouth wobbling even as she bit into her lower lip to disguise it. Cesar's belly dropped as if from a great height as something very cold lanced him. He'd just assumed... been so focused on how intense it had been for him... Even though he'd believed it had been the same for her, but she was so small...

He could feel tremors in Lexie's body now—as if she was experiencing a delayed reaction. Cesar moved and came up on one arm, cold terror trickling through him. 'Did I hurt you?'

Rapidly she shook her head and Cesar saw her eyes fill in earnest now, felt the tremors in her body getting stronger. Her cheeks paled. Was she going into some kind of shock?

Her body, which had felt so warm and languorous seconds before, now felt cold. Galvanised by increasing panic, Cesar gathered Lexie into his arms and stood up from the bed, taking her with him. She curled up against his chest, making something like bile fill him at the thought that he'd hurt her. She said nothing.

He walked into the bathroom and straight into the shower, where he turned on the powerful spray of hot water and stood them both under it. He felt Lexie gasp, her body curl even tighter into him, and he also felt those tremors increase as she started crying in earnest.

Her face was buried in his chest and her slim back was heaving with the force of her sobs as her hands pressed against him.

Cesar felt as if his chest was being ripped apart by bare hands. 'Lexie...*Dios*...please tell me...did I hurt you?'

She shook her head against him. The slimmest sliver of relief went through him. Cesar rested his back against the wall and wasn't even sure how long he stayed like that, under the powerful spray, while Lexie sobbed in his arms. He could still feel the power of the emotion running through her slim body.

Eventually the storm passed and she became still. They were surrounded in hot steam. She started to move, and then he heard a husky, rough-sounding, 'You can put me down. I'm okay.'

Reluctantly, even though his arms were stiff, Cesar let her down until she stood. She wouldn't look at him and he had to tip her chin up. When he saw those huge bruised eyes and her swollen mouth he had to curb his almost instantaneous reaction. *Again.* Already...

'Lexie...what...?'

She shook her head, came close, put her hands on his chest. 'You didn't hurt me...' Her voice sounded raw. 'The opposite. I promise.'

Cesar frowned as water ran in rivulets down their bodies, plastering their hair to their skulls. 'But...why?'

Lexie ducked her head, resting her forehead against him for a moment and making something incredibly alien flood through Cesar. Then she looked up again, 'I just... It's never been like that. That's all.'

Cesar had the distinct feeling that that *wasn't* all, but

something held him back from forcing her to explain. He hadn't hurt her. The relief was almost overwhelming.

'Come on,' he said gruffly. 'Let's get out.'

He turned off the water and stepped out, reaching back for Lexie. She emerged from the steam, taking his hand, and he couldn't stop his gaze from devouring those naked curves greedily. She was looking at him too, and Cesar had to stop himself from pressing her up against the shower wall and taking her there and then.

Instead he wrapped a towel around her and her hair. She stood as mute as a child and let him dry her off, and after he'd dried himself roughly he took her back into the bedroom.

He dropped his towel and gently took hers off and led her back to the bed. Her hair was damp but she didn't look inclined to dry it. He could see her eyes heavy with the need to sleep. Heavy after the outpouring of emotion that had left tentacles of panic inside him at the thought that he'd hurt her.

She crawled into the bed and lay down, and Cesar looked at her before getting in beside her. This was anathema to him—sharing a bed after lovemaking. But it was something he wasn't in a position to question right now.

Lexie burrowed straight into his arms, wrapping her legs around him, resting her head on his chest. Those soft abundant curves melted into him. His heart thudding unevenly, it was only when he could feel her body relax into sleep and her hold on him loosen that he was able to relax himself.

When Lexie woke up she opened her eyes and blinked at the dawn light coming in through long grand windows. She felt completely disorientated. Her body felt...different. Heavy. Lethargic. *Sated.* Hers...

She became aware of something moving steadily under

her cheek. *Cesar's chest*. She lifted her head and looked up to see him asleep. Dark stubble lined his jaw. And then her eye caught something else and she let out a small gasp of dismay.

A neat row of small teeth marks scored the flesh of his shoulder. And suddenly Lexie was back in that moment of such extreme pleasure that she'd had to bite him to keep from screaming.

She ducked her head again quickly, face burning. It all came back…every scorching moment. Taking him into her body had been far more momentous and emotional than she would ever have imagined it might be.

She'd cried like a baby.

Lexie cringed to think of how she'd curled up into his chest and sobbed. How he'd asked if he'd hurt her. Far from it. She felt almost guilty—as if she'd misled him by not telling him about herself. As if she'd taken something she only had half a right to. This man would never know the precious gift he'd unwittingly given her.

A sense of liberation from the dark past rushed up in a giddying sweep of emotion so physically acute that Lexie had to move or risk waking him. And she wasn't ready for that assessing gaze to land on her just yet.

Moving stealthily, she managed to extricate herself and climb out of the bed without disturbing Cesar, who lay in a louche, sexy sprawl. She couldn't help stopping for a moment and looking at him covetously. He was so beautiful…his skin a deep olive, his chest broad and powerful, and lower… Her face burned even hotter at the thought of how he'd felt moving inside her. So gentle but so powerful.

Emotion tightened like a fist around her heart. On first acquaintance with this man, she never could have imagined he'd have so many hidden depths, or have the capacity to be so…*considerate*.

Lexie immediately dismissed the direction of her

thoughts when a kind of panic seized her guts. She had to lock off her emotions. This was purely physical. She'd gone into this with eyes wide open. It was an affair. And when the time came she would walk away with her head held high.

Lexie grabbed up her things and crept out of the room. Once she was in her own room she had a shower, before donning faded comfy jeans and a V-necked cashmere top. She pulled her hair back into a ponytail and went to find the kitchen.

Lexie had found a radio station playing classical Spanish music and was blissfully unaware of the tall man resting his shoulder against the door, arms crossed, as she made breakfast.

It was only when she turned around to find some salt and pepper that she saw him and nearly jumped out of her skin.

He straightened. 'Sorry, I didn't mean to startle you.'

Lexie flushed, still not ready to see him. Already a hum was starting in her blood. 'You didn't…' She flushed some more. 'I mean, you did—but it's okay.'

He was bare-chested and wearing jeans with the top button open. Lexie nearly melted. Her body was unaccustomed to this overload of sensations and desires.

He came into the kitchen, right up to her, and growled softly, 'I woke up alone.'

'I just…I woke up and you were asleep,' Lexie stammered. 'I didn't want to disturb you.'

A look she couldn't identify came into his eyes and he said, 'You didn't.'

He bent then, and pressed his mouth to hers. In an instant she was on fire, her mouth opening under his, seeking more. When he pulled back she was breathing fast.

She was out of her depth. This whole morning-after thing was totally alien to her.

In a bid to try and disguise her discomfiture Lexie turned back to where she was frying some eggs and bacon, glancing over her shoulder. 'I hope you don't mind... I found some food in the fridge. Are you hungry?'

She was babbling now.

Cesar just leant back against the island in the kitchen and said huskily, 'I'm starving.'

But the look he sent up and down Lexie's body told her he didn't mean for food. She bit her lip and tried to ignore her body's reaction. Was this even normal?

Somehow she managed to make something resembling breakfast and coffee, and to serve it up without it ending up all over the floor.

The state-of-the-art kitchen in Cesar's apartment led into a large open-plan dining/living space. She sat down at the table there and noticed that there were Sunday papers, and—thankfully—that Cesar had put a top on.

He saw her glance at the papers and explained, 'The concierge drops them in if I'm here.'

Lexie spotted something that piqued her interest and pulled one of the more tabloid-looking papers out of the pile—only to realise that the press had managed to catch her and Cesar on their open-top bus tour.

There were also pictures of them walking hand in hand back to the apartment.

Something about that sent acute disappointment to her gut. It had been a spontaneous moment. This tainted the memory. She said faintly, 'I never imagined they could have known that we'd be doing that.'

Cesar took a sip of coffee and said, almost absent-mindedly, 'I called my assistant—told her to tip them off anonymously.'

Something cold slithered into Lexie's gut. She put down

her fork and looked at Cesar and brought up a dim recollection of him on his phone briefly at one stage on the bus.

'But....' Lexie was about to ask him *why* when she stopped herself. Of *course* he'd wanted to tip them off. They were meant to be courting the press—for both their benefits. Why waste an opportunity to document it?

'But...?' he asked.

She hated to think it, even to acknowledge it, but she felt betrayed. And she shouldn't be feeling that. Because if she did then it meant that Cesar had attained a significance for her that she had no control over.

She forced a smile and shook her head. 'But nothing. Of course you should have tipped them off. It was a good opportunity to let them see us.'

Cesar watched Lexie continuing to eat her breakfast and something twisted inside him. She looked so young, so innocent.

When he'd woken up alone in the bed his immediate reaction had been irritation that she'd left. He'd been about to go and find her when he'd remembered her tears, that incredible outpouring of emotion, and like a coward he'd stopped. Not sure if he was ready to face that searing blue gaze in the morning light.

The look in her eyes just now, though, made him feel like a heel. His own conscience mocked him. Making that call to his assistant yesterday had come out of a gut reaction to how Lexie's lit-up face and smile had made him feel. A gut reaction to doing something so out of his comfort zone. Cesar didn't *do* quirky, fun sightseeing tours with lovers. He didn't engage with the public. But he had—and moreover he'd found himself enjoying it.

He was dark and brooding, and most people ran a mile when they saw him. But not when he was with Lexie.

And that, frankly, had terrified him. So he'd called Mercedes and once he'd instructed her to alert the press he'd felt that he *hadn't* lost his mind completely.

Now, absurdly, he felt guilty.

Lexie was taking a sip of coffee, wiping her mouth, avoiding his eyes. Cesar reached out and took her hand. He saw her tense and that guilt intensified. *Damn her.*

Warily she looked at him.

Carefully Cesar said, 'Our becoming lovers was inevitable. Diverting the media is a beneficial consequence for both of us.'

Lexie blinked. Cesar saw how her expression became inscrutable, hidden.

'Of course. I know that. Don't worry, Cesar, I'm not some soft-hearted teenager who is weaving fantasies around a happy-ever-after scenario. I know that doesn't exist. Believe me.'

Something about the harshness of her tone caught at Cesar's chest, making it ache even as everything within him urged him to agree with her, to feel relieved.

She stood up to take their plates and Cesar caught her wrist, said gruffly, 'Leave it. My housekeeper will attend to it later, when we're gone.'

He tugged her towards him until she put down the plates and fell, resisting, into his lap.

She huffed out, 'What are you doing?'

The feel of her soft, lithe body against his made a lie of every one of Cesar's last words. All he could think about was how much he wanted this woman. But Lexie was stiff in his arms and that made him feel slightly desperate.

His hand was on her waist and he could feel a sliver of silky skin under her top. He explored underneath, over the indent of her naked waist and higher. Already he could feel the effect, the softening and relaxing of her body into his.

'Lexie…'

Slowly she turned her head to his, and for a moment

there was something unguarded in the depths of her eyes. Something very raw and pained. But it didn't make Cesar want to run.

His exploring hand came into contact with the bare swell of her breast. *No bra.* And just like that lust surged between them, red-hot and powerful. Their mouths connected, their kiss deepened, Lexie groaned softly and Cesar cupped the full weight of that breast in his hand.

Weakly he drowned out the clamouring voices in his head that told him he was deluding himself if he believed that he was half as in control of this as he would have Lexie believe.

CHAPTER EIGHT

'LET'S GO AGAIN, folks.'

Lexie clenched her jaw. This was the thirteenth take, and if she fluffed her lines one more time more than one crew member would want to wring her neck. Including herself. The director called *action* and by some miracle Lexie managed to get through the dialogue with no mishaps.

There was an audible sigh of relief around the set. Everyone was tired. It was the end of the third week and fatigue was setting in. The prospect of another week here and then two weeks in London stretched like a never-ending horizon line.

As they called that scene complete and started to set up for the next one Lexie was whisked back to the unit base for a costume-change. She relished the time to try and gather her scattered and fragmented thoughts.

Since the previous cataclysmic weekend, and their return to the *castillo* from Madrid on Sunday, Lexie had been avoiding Cesar at every opportunity. It didn't help that he was almost constantly on set—hence her fluffed lines and general state of being flustered. But today he hadn't shown up, and that had nearly been worse.

Lexie was terrified that she'd gone and fallen for the first man who had come along and kissed her whole body awake—much like Sleeping Beauty in the fairy tale.

That was why she'd been avoiding Cesar all week. She

felt as if she wasn't in control of these new and overwhelming desires. It was like having a car and not really knowing how to drive it—being afraid that if she got behind the wheel it would careen off the road and cause mayhem and destruction.

She felt feverish, excited. Exactly like the soft-hearted teenager she'd mocked only days ago.

That weekend he'd only had to pull her onto his lap and kiss her before she'd been reduced to a puddle of lust, letting him take her back to bed and make love to her again and again. Showing her the heights her body could attain with just the barest sweep of his clever fingers against her body's core.

He had no idea who he was dealing with. The dark secrets Lexie harboured. But every time Cesar touched her she felt more and more exposed—as if sooner or later she wouldn't be able to stop it all tumbling out. Baring her soul to him.

So she'd been avoiding him. Like a coward. Even though all she could think about and dream about and yearn for was him.

It was affecting her work. And it didn't help that one scene in particular was due to be shot at the beginning of the following week and Lexie was dreading it, but unable to say anything to anyone about it.

After her dresser had left Lexie waited for the call to go back to set, pacing up and down her trailer, repeating her lines, trying to force all other thoughts out of her head.

When a knock came on her trailer door she said distractedly, 'I'll be out in a minute,' assuming that it was the call for set. But then the door opened and Lexie whirled around, copious amounts of silken layers rustling as she did so, only to see Cesar coming up the steps and entering.

Immediately the relatively big space was tiny. He closed the door behind him. He looked dark, gorgeous. Intent.

Lexie was breathless, and it only had a little to do with her costume. 'You shouldn't be here—they'll be calling for me in a minute.'

Cesar crossed his arms. '*Here* seems to be the only place I can find you without you avoiding me or hiding in your room.'

Lexie flushed, her whole body tingling just to be near him. She couldn't deny the sheer excitement that gripped her, the anticipation at the look in Cesar's eye. Especially when his gaze dropped to the swells of her breasts, made even more provocative than usual in the dress.

Lord, she wanted him right now. *Here*. Like some lurid parody of the stories she'd heard of actors and actresses behaving badly while shooting on location.

Cesar came towards her and Lexie had nowhere to escape to. He wrapped an arm around her waist and pulled her into him. Her body sang and, bizarrely, something inside her calmed. She felt more centred.

'Why have you been avoiding me all week?' he growled.

'Work...I need to concentrate on my work,' Lexie blurted out weakly.

His eyes flashed. 'Well, you're singularly to blame for *me* not being able to concentrate on a single thing.'

'Really?' Inordinate pleasure snaked through Lexie to hear that. To imagine this stern, unflappable man being distracted because of her. She felt like smiling.

'I don't play games, Lexie.'

She blanched. 'You think...you think I'm playing some *game*?'

His jaw was set, stern. Her belly swooped.

'Cesar...I'm not playing a game... I was avoiding you because last weekend... It's just been a long time for me.' *Try for ever,* said a small voice, but she blocked it out. 'I'm not used to this—I don't have *affairs*.'

Flustered, she ducked her head. Cesar put a finger to her chin to tip her face back up.

His gaze dropped to her cleavage and his voice was rough. '*Dios*...do you know what it does to me to see you in these dresses?' His eyes met hers again and his arm tightened around her. 'Come to my apartment this evening.'

Resistance was futile. Lexie felt herself dissolving, aching to say *yes*, let him take control so she didn't have to think or analyse. Just *be*.

'Okay.' She smiled, unable to keep it in.

Cesar was about to kiss her when a knock came on the door and a PA called out, 'Lexie, they're ready for you.'

Cesar stopped and Lexie almost groaned. 'Okay, thanks,' she called back.

Then he smiled, and it was wicked. 'I'll cook dinner. Come by when you've wrapped. Bring a weekend bag.'

Lexie almost rolled her eyes, 'My room is in the *castillo*. If I need anything surely I can just—?'

Cesar cut her off. 'Just...do it.'

'Okay,' Lexie said again, her smile turning wry at his autocratic tone.

She let Cesar lead her out to where her driver was waiting in the car to take her back to the set.

The following day Lexie grumbled good-naturedly, '*Why* can't you tell me where we're going?'

Cesar stopped abruptly and Lexie almost careened into him. He caught her hands and held them. The breeze had mussed up his hair. He looked vital, and so gorgeous that she sighed with pure appreciation. He looked darker too, all dressed in black.

He was mock stern. 'Just do as you're told.'

Lexie saw a staff member carrying their bags to a waiting helicopter. It was sitting on a landing pad at the back of the *castillo*.

Cesar had woken her early that morning and she'd stretched like a satisfied cat amongst his very tousled sheets before she'd even really realised the enormity of where she was.

In Cesar's bed, in his private apartment. After a night of lovemaking that had almost brought her to tears again. She'd only held them back with gritted teeth, determined not to let him see her get so emotional again.

But she couldn't help it. With every touch, every kiss, this man was rebuilding the very fabric of her soul. A fabric that had been torn apart brutally years before.

As instructed, she'd packed some things the previous evening and had gone to his apartment after work to find him waiting for her, busy in his kitchen making dinner. The sight had been so incongruous and so...*sexy* that Lexie had struggled to affect a nonchalance she hadn't felt.

Before she could say anything else Cesar took her by the hand and led her to the helicopter, bundling her inside. Lexie gave up trying to figure out where they were going and did as she was told, putting on earphones and buckling up.

Cesar leant over from his seat to help her just as the rotor blades started up outside, and adrenalin and excitement kicked in her belly.

He grinned at her. 'Don't worry—you'll like it, I promise.' And then he pressed a swift kiss to her mouth and sat back.

Lexie scowled at him, hating that his grin made her heart clench and that he could so easily affect her. But then her mind emptied as the chopper rose smoothly into the air and she saw the *castillo* drop away underneath them.

Cesar had obviously asked the pilot to take a tour of the estate, and he pointed out vineyards and more land than she had ever realised belonged to him. It was truly mind-boggling. And sobering to realise the extent of his responsibilities.

Then they were banking and heading away from where the sun had risen only a short while before. Lexie was transfixed by the changing landscape underneath them as they passed over low mountains and rivers.

Eventually she could see that the sparse countryside was making way for more built-up areas. Cesar took her hand and pointed out of the main window of the helicopter. She could make out a smudge of blue...*the sea*?

She glanced at him and he smiled. One of those rare smiles that made her want to smile back like a loon. She could see that they were flying over what had to be a city. The rooftops were terra-cotta, glinting in the sun. She saw a very majestic-looking castle on a hill.

They seemed, impossibly, to be heading right for the city centre. Lexie could see a bridge spanning a huge river, and the way the city was spread out on hills. It didn't look especially modern. There were trams and beautiful old crumbling buildings covered in coloured tiles.

She gasped and turned to Cesar and shouted over the noise, 'Lisbon?'

He nodded. So that's why he'd told her to pack her passport. A rush of incredible emotion and gratitude filled Lexie. She remembered standing in his study that day and exclaiming with a feeling of panic that she wanted to visit Madrid, Salamanca and Lisbon.

So far he'd taken her to all of them.

The helicopter set down on the rooftop of a building and Cesar helped her out. Lexie realised it was a hotel when the staff greeted them and led them inside where solicitous customs officials were waiting for them to check their passports. Cesar took her hand once they were done and she sent him a quick, dry look. 'No queues for you?'

Cesar smiled. 'My name, Da Silva, isn't strictly Span-

ish in origin. It comes from a very distant Portuguese an-
cestor. So I'm allowed…certain liberties…'

Lexie all but rolled her eyes as one of the staff got
Cesar's attention. She'd just bet he was allowed untold
liberties for the promise of his favour and business oppor-
tunities. The fact that he was obviously a regular visitor
to Lisbon told her that he didn't take advantage of their
respect and that made her feel soft inside.

They went one floor down and were shown into the
most sumptuous suite of rooms Lexie had ever seen.

She explored on her own and found a terrace outside
the bedroom's French doors. She went out. The view was
astounding. She could see the huge imposing castle up on
a nearby hill, lots of steep streets with distinctive yellow
trams. And then what had to be the River Tagus, spanned
by a massive bridge.

She felt a presence behind her and then arms came
around her, hands resting by hers on the rail. Lexie shut
her eyes for a second at the way her body wanted to melt,
and when Cesar pressed close behind her she *did* melt into
him, blocking out the voices screaming *Danger! Danger!*

One of his hands disappeared and she felt her hair being
tugged back gently, so her neck was bared. Breath feath-
ered there and then she felt his mouth, warm and firm.
Lexie's hands tightened on the rail and the view became
blurry.

She turned around to face him and looked up. His eyes
were heavy-lidded, full of something dark and hot. A pulse
throbbed between Lexie's legs.

'I have a whole agenda laid out for you today, Miss
Anderson.'

Lexie arched a brow and tried to be cool. 'Oh, you do?'

Cesar nodded, and took some of her bright hair between two fingers. He tugged gently again and his eyes
rose to hers.

'And right now I have something very specific in mind.'
Lexie was already breathless. 'You do...?'

'Yes.'

And then, with devastating precision, Cesar's mouth closed over hers and Lexie didn't care where she was in the world as long as she was right in this moment.

'A nightcap?'

Lexie looked at Cesar and nodded. 'That'd be nice, thanks.'

She watched as he turned and went to the drinks cabinet, her eyes devouring his tall, lean form sheathed in a dark trousers and a light shirt. He'd already shrugged off his jacket.

Lexie was reeling after the day. Not wanting Cesar to see how overwhelmed she was, she made her way out to the terrace that was accessible through the living room too. She heard the faint sound of a mobile and Cesar's deep tones as he answered.

A quiver of relief went through her—a moment alone, to try and assimilate everything. She sucked in the evening air, hoping it might cool her hot cheeks. They'd felt permanently hot since Cesar had made love to her that morning.

Afterwards, when she'd been sated and replete, he hadn't let her burrow back under the covers as she'd wanted to. He'd all but washed and dressed her, picking out a pretty shirt and jeans, sneakers.

They'd left the hotel and a car had taken them up to the impressive St George's castle, with its breathtaking views of the city. Peacocks had strutted on the paths, fanning their colourful tails much to the delight of the tourists.

Then, as if reading Lexie's mind, he'd taken her on one of the old yellow trams down a steep hill. It had been so packed that Cesar had pulled her into his body in front of him, arms wrapped tight around her. By the time he'd pulled her out at another stop she had been thoroughly turned on.

She'd found herself being led though a dizzying labyrinth of ancient streets. Cesar had explained that it was the Alfama—the old Arabic quarter.

Beautiful murals decorated walls at the ends of alleyways, little children darted dark heads out of tiny windows and called, *'Bom dia!'* Washing hung on lines between houses.

They'd had lunch there, on a tiny terrace overlooking the river. Afterwards they'd wandered some more, Lexie's hand tightly in Cesar's. At one point she had tugged gently, and when he'd looked at her she'd asked, 'No paparazzi?'

Something had flashed across his face but he'd smiled and said, 'No. Not here.'

Something very dangerous had infused Lexie's blood to think that here they were truly anonymous. That Cesar hadn't automatically thought of the bigger agenda.

Dangerous.

The car had reappeared then, as if by magic, and had taken them to see the stunning sixteenth-century monastery where Vasco Da Gama was buried in Belem. Afterwards Cesar had pointed to a blue-canopied shop nearby, where a queue literally about a mile long waited patiently.

They'd joined the back of it. Lexie had looked at Cesar, but he'd said enigmatically, 'Wait and see. Then you'll understand why all these people are here.'

Eventually, when they'd reached the shop itself, Cesar had spoken in flawless Portuguese. He'd handed Lexie what looked like a small custard tart.

'Taste it,' Cesar had urged as they'd found stools in the heaving shop with its beautiful ornate interior.

Lexie had obediently bitten into the flaky pastry and the smooth warm custard had melted on her tongue. She'd groaned her appreciation, much as everyone else had.

When she'd been able to speak again she'd said, 'That was probably one of the best tarts I've ever tasted in my life.'

A smug Cesar had just said, 'See?'

And then they'd queued again for more.

After they'd taken a circuitous sightseeing route back to the hotel, instead of leading her up to the suite Cesar had taken Lexie down to the spa, where he'd consulted in Portuguese with the receptionist, who had gone bright pink and giggly. Lexie might almost have felt sorry for her if she hadn't been feeling a disturbing rise of something else. *Jealousy.*

Cesar had turned to her. 'See you in a couple of hours.' And after pressing a swift kiss to her mouth he'd left Lexie there, gaping at his retreating form.

Two women had emerged and Lexie had been taken in hand—literally. The full works of an all-over beauty treatment, followed by a full body massage.

Then, when she'd floated back to the suite, Cesar had been waiting with champagne, and once Lexie had changed into the dark pink off-the-shoulder dress she'd brought with her they'd gone to dinner.

And now...now...Lexie took in the sparkling view of one of the oldest cities in Europe and felt overwhelmed. No more in control of her emotions than she had been ever since they'd queued a second time for the glorious *pasteis de natas* in Belem. When Cesar had looked so carefree and years younger.

Conversely, it had reminded Lexie that she harboured dark secrets, and they were rising up within her now— because she was going to be coming face to face with a very personal old scar on set the following week. The thought of it terrified her, and she knew she was feeling more vulnerable about it because being with Cesar...being intimate for the first time…had ripped away some vital layer of protection.

'Sorry, I had to take that call.'

Lexie tensed at Cesar's deep voice. He came alongside her and handed her a small glass of port. She forced a smile and tipped it towards him after sniffing it appreciatively. 'Appropriate—given we're in the land where port is made.'

Cesar inclined his head. He looked absurdly suave and gorgeous this evening. Tall and imposing. Yet with that very definite edge of virile masculine energy.

Lexie took a quick sip of her drink. It was smooth and luxurious. Her feeling of vulnerability and the darkness on her soul made her want to avoid Cesar's far too incisive gaze. Even now he was regarding her speculatively. She felt raw after the day, and on some perverse level she almost felt angry with him—for charming her, for making her fall for him.

A rogue desire to crack that impenetrable façade he wore so well made her ask, 'So how come you're not married…?'

Lexie immediately wanted to claw the words back. Regretting the impulse.

Cesar's gaze narrowed predictably and Lexie squirmed, cursing herself. Thinking frantically of a way to save herself, she sought to mitigate it by saying lightly, 'You're a catch. I mean you have all your own teeth, your breath isn't bad. You own property…'

Somehow Lexie was afraid she hadn't fooled him. Her voice had sounded too breathy, slightly desperate. She took another sip of the port.

But when she looked back at him he was smiling wryly. 'No one's ever mentioned the boon of having my own teeth before.'

No, thought Lexie, she'd bet they hadn't. They'd probably looked at him and seen a walking, talking dollar sign.

Inexplicable anger rose up within her to think of women seeing him as a target, and then just as quickly dissolved. Cesar was so cynical that he would never be taken for that kind of a fool.

Suddenly loath to think that he might consider *her* a vulture like that, she said quietly, 'Thank you. Seriously, this day has been…amazing. I never expected it.'

Something painful gripped her inside. Their time was finite.

Not wanting to think about that, she figured she had nothing to lose so she dived in, telling herself she wasn't genuinely curious. 'Have you ever come close? To being married?'

Cesar tensed. His fingers tightened fractionally on his glass. Then the line of his mouth flattened. 'I was abandoned at an early age and then left in the hands of two people who were little better than uninterested caretakers. They resented the fact that my blood was not pure. That experience hardly left me with the qualifications to create a warm, inviting atmosphere conducive to family and such frivolous things.'

Lexie's insides clenched in rejection of that. Creating a family, a home, was not frivolous. Cesar's words, however, had been emphatic. She realised something about herself then, in a blinding flash of clarity: on some fundamental level she hadn't given up hope for herself. She hoped that some day she might have a second chance and her own rather dismal experience of what a family was could be proved to be the exception rather than the rule.

'Your half-brothers…' she offered huskily. 'They looked happy in the wedding pictures.'

Cesar's jaw tightened. 'They're different. They had a different upbringing, different perspectives.'

Lexie thought of his grandmother, cruelly making him

cut out and paste pictures of them growing up with their mother—*his* mother. Together.

'They had your mother… But I wonder if it was any easier or better for them just because she was there?'

'Perhaps—perhaps not,' Cesar said, but it rang hollow.

Lexie wanted to slide her arm around him but didn't. 'Are you going to see them again?'

He glanced at her and his face was hard. As it had been when he'd looked at the portraits of his grandparents.

'I have nothing in common with them. Especially not now.'

He turned to face her more fully and Lexie almost shivered at the frost in his eyes.

'I made a decision a long time ago never to marry and have children.'

'Why?' Lexie breathed, not liking how that declaration seemed to affect her physically. How it felt as if he was giving her a distinct message.

'Because I vowed that the *castillo* is no place for a child. The legacy of my family is tainted, built on obsessive greed. Snobbery. When I die the *castillo* will be left to the local town and they can do what they like with it. And all the money will go to various charities and trusts. That's what I'm building it up for now.'

'But…' Lexie searched wildly for a way to penetrate the cool shell that surrounded Cesar. 'You said yourself that you wanted to renovate the *castillo*, but…why bother? Why not just leave it behind now?'

Cesar looked at her then, and for a second Lexie saw bleakness in those green depths. A bleakness that resonated in her because she knew what it felt like herself.

'Because…' he was grim '…it's in my damn blood like some kind of poison.'

Lexie was stunned into silence. She didn't like the way she wanted to do something to comfort Cesar. Touch him.

And even though he was only inches away it felt as if a chasm yawned between them.

Huskily she said, 'I'm sorry. I shouldn't have said anything.'

His mouth tipped up but it was a parody of a smile, a million miles away from the smiles she'd seen earlier.

'What about you, Lexie? Do you wish for a cottage with a white picket fence and a gaggle of cherubic children?'

For a second Lexie felt nothing. The words seemed to hang suspended in the air between them. But then it was as if a roaring flood was approaching and gathering speed from a long way off. *Pain*. Incredible pain.

A kaleidoscope of images bombarded her—a tiny baby, crying lustily. Nurses with rough hands and judgemental looks. Officials. And then…nothing. Silence. More pain.

'Lexie?'

She blinked. Cesar was watching her, his eyes narrowing. Face stark. From somewhere she found a brittle smile and said through the ball of emotion growing in her chest, 'You forgot the dog…there's a dog there too.'

'Ah…yes, of course. No idyllic picture would be complete without a dog.'

Cesar put down his glass and took Lexie's from her too. He reached for her with both hands and pulled her into his body. Lexie felt cold, and she shivered lightly. She desperately wanted to drive away the chill and feel warm again. She desperately wanted to blank out the dark images she'd just seen.

Coming up on her tiptoes, Lexie reached up and brought her arms around Cesar's neck, pressing her whole body against his. She saw the flare in his eyes and felt herself start to thaw from the inside out.

'Kiss me, Cesar.'

Cesar smiled briefly before a look of almost feral intent crossed his face. He moved his hands up to Lexie's face.

The kiss was fierce and passionate, and before Lexie lost all ability to think clearly she knew that they were both running away from the demons nipping at their heels. This time, though, it didn't feel like kinship—it felt bleak.

Much later Cesar lay awake in the dark room. Traces of the constriction in his chest brought on by Lexie's questions were still there, faintly. Even though his body hummed with much more pleasurable sensations.

She was curled into him now, her naked curves keeping him at a level of near constant arousal. If it wasn't so damned intoxicating he could almost resent her for her effect on him.

Her breath was feathering softly across his chest, light and even, and her hair was soft and silky. One hand lay right over the centre of his chest, where he'd felt the constriction most keenly earlier.

'So how come you're not married?'

Other women had asked him that question with a definite look in their eyes. Lexie hadn't had that look. He never talked to anyone about his upbringing, but he seemed to be incapable of holding it in whenever those huge blue eyes were trained on him.

He'd told her...*everything.* He'd never even articulated his plans for the *castillo* to his friend Juan. He'd never told another soul. And when he'd told her something incredibly bleak had hit him. Bleak enough to drive him to taunt her, ask her if she pictured herself in that idyllic scenario.

And she'd looked for a moment as if he'd run a knife right through her belly. Pale. Stricken. Shocked. Clearly the thought was anathema to her, even though she'd joked about a dog.

Cesar went cold in the bed beside Lexie as something slid home inside him. The joke was on him, because for the first time in his life he was aware of a yearning sensation, a yearning for something he'd always believed to be utterly beyond his reach.

The following morning Lexie woke up alone in the bed. She sagged back against the pillows with not a little relief. Images from the night flooded her head and her cheeks reddened even as a tight knot of tension made her belly cramp.

She'd been able to drive away the demons for the night, but now they were back. The conversation with Cesar replayed in her head. The bleakness she'd felt when he'd spoken about the *castillo*, about leaving it behind so no child would have to endure what he had.

It shouldn't be affecting Lexie like this. If anything it should be inciting a sense of protection within her. A sense that as long as she could count on Cesar's obviously deeply rooted cynicism then she would be okay too.

But she couldn't keep fooling herself. That discussion with Cesar had told Lexie that she wasn't half as cynical as she'd always believed she was. It had told her that at a very deep core level she *did* harbour a fantasy. A fantasy of family and security and happiness. Fulfilment. It might not be dressed up in a vision of a cute cottage with a white picket fence and a dog and children, but it wasn't far off.

And it made Lexie feel physically ill, almost as if she'd betrayed herself, to realise that. She'd been betrayed in the worst way possible by the very people who should have loved and protected her. And she'd always vowed to herself that she'd never allow that to happen again.

She'd vowed it. But deep down she hadn't wanted to become that hard inside.

Lexie could see now that that was why she'd allowed herself to believe she could trust Jonathan Saunders, even briefly. Even then she'd been trying to prove to herself that she could trust again. That she could believe that she wouldn't be betrayed. But he *had* betrayed her. And that should have proved to her that she'd been right all along not to trust. It should have shored up her defences. Made her even stronger.

But it hadn't.

Because Lexie knew that any illusion of feeling in control of what was happening between her and Cesar Da Silva was exactly that. An illusion. And this man had the power to show her the true extent of how flimsy her defences had always been.

CHAPTER NINE

'WOULD YOU MIND if we returned to the *castillo* this morning? Something's come up that I have to attend to in the vineyards.'

Lexie was in the bedroom and had just finished dressing in the jeans she'd worn the day before and a stripy Breton top. For a second Cesar's words didn't even compute because she was just drinking him in, looking impossibly handsome in jeans and a light wool sweater.

Then the words registered and relief rocked through her. She'd been dreading facing Cesar so soon after her recent revelations.

'No,' she said quickly—too quickly. 'I don't mind at all. There's some heavy scenes next week so I'd appreciate some time to prepare…'

Anxiety at the prospect of what lay ahead for her gripped her again.

Cesar crossed his arms and lounged against the door. Instantly Lexie's skin prickled with awareness. She could feel her nipples drawing into tight buds. Even more reason why she would relish some space from this man…

'You don't have to sound so eager.'

She blushed and glanced away for a second, feeling churlish. 'It's not that I want to leave…you've been so generous…'

Cesar closed the distance between them so fast her head spun. He looked stern. 'You don't have to thank me.'

Lexie said weakly, 'Yes, I do… It's polite.'

'I don't want your politeness,' Cesar growled softly. 'I want you.'

He cupped the back of her head and kissed her. Lexie clung to his arms to stop her legs from buckling.

When he drew back she opened her eyes. *Lord,* she could barely breathe.

'Maybe I can convince them they don't need me,' Cesar said roughly.

It took a second for his meaning to sink in and then, despite the lurch in her chest, Lexie said hurriedly, 'No, you should go back. And I *do* need to prepare for next week.'

'You're staying with me in my apartment, though.'

She opened her mouth to object and saw the glint of determination in Cesar's eyes. She sighed, feeling weak. 'Okay.'

Much later that night Cesar finally returned to his apartment in the *castillo*. He was irritated and frustrated. The problem in the vineyards had been more complicated than he'd thought, and then he'd been waylaid by his house manager and that had evolved into a long impromptu meeting about the renovations Cesar was embarking on. Renovations that were now taking on a new resonance—as if something had shifted inside him with regards to his long-term plans for the *castillo*.

But he didn't want to think of that. All he wanted *was to see Lexie.* His apartment was quiet. Empty. When he considered for a second that she might well have gone back to her own rooms the rise of an even deeper frustration made him clench his jaw.

But, no… He saw her sneakers, thrown off near the couch where a low light was burning. Cesar walked over and his chest grew tight when he saw Lexie fast asleep. Her top had risen up, revealing a sliver of pale soft belly. One arm was flung over her head, the other was just below her breasts.

He came closer and wasn't even really aware of the way the irritation and frustration he'd been feeling moments before had just dissolved away. To be replaced by a different kind of frustration. A hunger.

He spotted the earphones of her mp3 player in her ears, the wires leading to the device. And that tightness was more acute as he thought of her dyslexia and how hard it must have been for her to overcome its challenges along the way.

As if aware of his intense scrutiny, she opened those huge blue eyes. It took a second for them to focus and then Lexie scrambled up, her cheeks pink.

'Oh, my God, what time is it?'

Cesar came down on the edge of the couch and pinned her with his arms. She lay back. She looked tousled and delicious and sexy as hell.

'It's way past your bedtime.'

She smiled and an incredible lightness infused Cesar. Addictive, seductive...

'Is it now? What are you going to do about it?'

Cesar said sternly, 'I'm going to make sure you go to bed right now and tuck you in myself.'

He stood up and reached for Lexie, swinging her into his arms, relishing the way she snuggled into his chest. Relishing even more the way her mouth unerringly found his neck and started pressing kisses there. Open-mouthed kisses, so that he could feel the tip of that wicked tongue.

Lexie sank back onto the bed and Cesar loomed over her, pulling off his top with one graceful move. She was still in a delicious half-dream haze. She didn't even have to be awake for him to have an effect on her.

But then, like a dream that became clearer on waking, the darkness of the material she'd been studying in the script came back to her. It made her mood change in an instant, dousing desire. She recalled too that just before she'd woken she'd been having disturbing dreams. Almost nightmares. And it was no wonder.

Cesar came down over her on his arms and just like that Lexie froze under him. In that instant she felt tainted, *damaged*. She could see now that the exhilaration of becoming more intimate with Cesar had helped her to forget for a moment who she really was. What had happened to her. The sheer extent of the dark secrets she harboured.

Right then it felt as if a chasm yawned between them. He wouldn't ever want to know who she really was. Why would he? This was just an affair. Fun. Lighthearted. Lexie felt anything *but* lighthearted. She felt acutely alone. As if she carried the weight of the world on her shoulders.

Cesar lifted a hand as if to touch her and Lexie flinched violently. Everything in her was screaming to get away *now*—before he could seduce her so much that she found herself spilling out all the awful ugliness that had no place here.

He stopped. 'Lexie…?'

Lexie scrambled out from under Cesar's arms and stood up by the bed, her whole body cold. Numb. Cesar was looking at her as if she'd grown two heads. Galvanised by panic, Lexie found her bag and started throwing things in.

'What are you doing?'

She shoved the blouse she'd worn the previous day into the bag, her belly swooping at the thought of that day. How perfect it had been. It felt as if it had happened to another person now. A person who *didn't* have the awful memories that were bombarding her right now.

'I'm going back to my own room.'

She picked up her bag but Cesar caught her arm. He was shaking his head, incredulous. 'What on earth is going on?'

She pulled her arm free and backed away, torn by the sense of increasing panic she felt and also by something much more disturbing: the desire to throw down the bag and launch herself into Cesar's arms, ask him just to hold her, to reassure her that she could feel safe with him. But that was not what he was interested in—Lexie being vulnerable. He'd run a mile.

Then he stopped looking incredulous. He folded his arms. 'I told you before that I don't play games, Lexie.'

Lexie felt sad. 'I'm not playing a game. I just can't do this right now. I need...some space.'

For a long second Cesar just regarded her, and then his face became unreadable. He stepped back and said coolly, 'By all means, Lexie, take all the space you need.'

Lexie gripped her bag and turned and walked out of the bedroom, and out of Cesar's apartment, adrenalin coursing through her system. When she got back to her own room it felt desolate. And then she realised with a sense of dread that *she* felt desolate.

The truth was that she was damaged and broken inside. For a brief moment in time she'd believed that she had somehow been miraculously cured. But she hadn't really. And this minor meltdown had just proved it to her.

'I need some space.' Cesar glowered so fiercely that his house manager saw him coming and scuttled out of sight. Those words had been eating away at him like poison for two days now.

One minute Lexie had been supine on his bed, flushed and sexy, huge eyes all but eating him up...and the next she'd become a different person. Cold. Stark. *Dios*, she'd flinched as if he might hurt her.

His skin prickled. He hadn't liked that feeling. And he

hadn't liked to acknowledge how feral she'd made him feel. When she'd said she needed space it had been like a punch to his gut.

The thought that she might have even glimpsed a tiny part of how ravenous she made him feel had made him go cold all over. He'd had to step back to stop himself from acting on the visceral impulse to prove her words to be a lie.

But even now he could remember the look in her eyes. It had been panicked. And he couldn't understand why.

The film unit was due to head back to London at the end of the week and Cesar was acutely aware of the fact— much to his chagrin. Especially when he'd set out at the very beginning to avoid getting involved at all costs.

For two days he'd deliberately avoided going near where they were shooting, in an old abandoned wing of the *castillo*. But today he found himself heading there even before he'd consciously taken the decision. The fact that he *needed* to see Lexie only put him into an even more foul humour.

Cesar saw the usual cluster of people as he got closer to the set—crew hanging around, waiting for someone to call for them urgently.

They nodded to him now. Said hello. He managed some civil responses. When he got closer he saw that the door to the set was closed. And there was a hushed air. He asked the third assistant director if they were shooting.

The young man shook his head and Cesar made to go onto the set, but the man stopped him. 'You can't go in there, Mr Da Silva.'

Cesar chafed at the obstruction. His need to see Lexie was like a burr under his skin now. 'Why not?' he demanded.

'It's a closed set. They're doing the rape scene. Essential crew only.'

The rape scene.

Cesar didn't know why, but he suddenly felt a chill in his blood. He looked around and saw the video assistant in the corner, with his wall of monitors which showed whatever the camera was seeing inside the room. Usually there would be a couple of producers or some crew watching the scenes, but today there was no one.

He went over and sat down. Just as he realised that he couldn't hear what they were saying the video assistant handed him some earphones. Cesar put them on and hunched forward.

They were about to shoot. The director was talking to Lexie and to Rogan, the male lead. Cesar's breath hitched when he saw her. Her hair was down, tousled, and she was wearing some kind of diaphanous white gown. It was open at the front, as if it had been ripped, and he could see the ripe curve of her breast.

And then the director disappeared, leaving Lexie and Rogan on the screen. The first assistant director called out the instructions to shoot and then the director called *action.*

Rogan grabbed Lexie by the arms and shook her, spittle flying from his mouth as he said crude, horrific things. She looked tiny and vulnerable. She was pleading with him. But he wouldn't listen. Then he brutally turned her and shoved her down on the bed, pulling her gown up over her thighs, undoing himself before he pressed himself into her, grunting like an animal.

The camera went close in on Lexie's face, pushed down onto the bed. Rogan's big hand was on the back of her head, holding her down. Her eyes were blank.

Cesar heard *cut.* But all he could really hear was the roaring of blood in his head. He wanted to move but he was paralysed.

On some rational level he knew it wasn't real. That it was just acting. He could see Rogan helping Lexie up. The

actor looked faintly traumatised. Lexie looked impossibly
pale, and sort of glassy-eyed. A shiver of foreboding went
down Cesar's spine. He knew that it had obviously been
a traumatic scene to shoot, but there was something else
going on—he could feel it.

But then they were going again, and he heard the camera assistant say, 'Scene One Hundred, Take Twenty.'

Cesar pulled off the earphones and looked at the video
guy incredulously. 'They've done this *nineteen* times?'

The man gulped. 'Yes, sir. We've been doing this scene
all day from different angles. This is the last shot, but he's
milking it.'

Cesar felt rage building inside him. The camera was
close up on Lexie's face again and he saw a tear roll out
of her eye and down one cheek. She hadn't cried last time.

Something rose up inside Cesar—something he couldn't
even articulate. An overwhelming need to get to her. He
surged to his feet, almost knocking over the wall of monitors. He stormed to the door of the set, swatting the pro-
testing third AD aside.

He opened the door just as the camera assistant was
saying, 'Scene One Hundred, Take Twenty-One.'

'Enough.' Cesar's voice cracked out like a whip.

Lexie turned her head and looked at Cesar. He saw only
those huge bruised blue eyes, and something in their
depths…a mute appeal. She wasn't acting any more. He
knew it without even knowing how.

He walked straight over and scooped her up into his
arms, and for the first time in two days he felt slightly
sane again.

The director was standing up now, blustering. 'What
the hell are you doing, Da Silva? You can't just barge in
here like this.'

Cesar stopped in the act of turning around. Lexie was

far too slight a weight in his arms as he said coldly, 'You're on my property. I can do whatever the hell I want.'

'But we haven't got the shot yet.'

Even icier now, Cesar said, 'If you haven't managed to get it yet then perhaps you shouldn't be directing.'

He was barely aware of a suppressed snigger from one of the crew as he strode out of the room, Lexie curled into his chest, her head tucked down. It reminded him of how she'd curled into his chest after making love that first time. When she'd cried like a baby.

He carried her all the way to his apartment and took her into his bedroom. He sat down on the edge of the bed, still holding her. He was shaking from the adrenalin and anger coursing through his system.

After a long time, she moved in his arms. But she wouldn't look at him. She just said, in a quiet voice, 'I need to have a shower.'

Cesar got up and deposited her gently on the side of the bed, crouching down. Finally she met his gaze but her eyes were flat. As if she didn't see him. A shard of ice pierced him inside.

Reluctantly he left her to go and turn on the shower. When he came out she was standing, albeit shakily. 'Do you need help?' he asked.

She shook her head and went in, closing the door behind her. Cesar restrained himself from following her, making sure she was all right. The shower ran for long minutes.

Eventually it stopped. Lexie was so long coming out that Cesar was about to knock on the door when it opened. She was wrapped in his towelling robe. It swamped her. Her hair was damp and hung in long golden tendrils over her shoulders.

He handed her a glass of brandy. 'Here—you should drink some of this.'

Lexie wrinkled her nose, but she took it and sipped at it before handing it back. Cesar put it down on a nearby table. He felt unaccountably ill-equipped to know what to do. What to say.

'You shouldn't have done that.'

She was looking at him with her chin tilted up and Cesar arched a brow. 'Would you prefer to be back there doing Take Thirty right now?'

She paled so dramatically that Cesar reached out and put his hands on her arms.

'No,' he said grimly, leading her out to the living area and guiding her to sit down on the couch. 'I didn't think so.'

Lexie seemed impossibly tiny and fragile sitting on the big couch. Cesar stood over her and crossed his arms, because even now all he wanted to do was touch her. *I need space.* He cursed silently.

'So, are you going to tell me what's going on?'

Lexie glanced up at Cesar and then away again quickly. He was so…implacable. Determined. Stern. The numb shell that had surrounded her for the past two days was finally breaking apart.

When Cesar had burst onto the set and she'd seen him… He would never know the depth of the gratitude she'd felt. Because on some level she'd always needed to know that someone might have saved her.

She forced herself to look at him. 'Why did you do that?'

Cesar paced back and forth now, energy sparking off his tall, lean body. His mouth was tight. 'I don't know, to be honest. But when I saw you…I could tell something was wrong.' He shook his head, stopped pacing. 'You weren't acting, Lexie.'

Something huge inside her shifted to know that he'd

intuited something was wrong. 'No, I wasn't acting…not by the end.'

Cesar pulled a chair over to sit in front of her. Lexie gazed at him. Remembered how good it had felt when he'd swept her up into his arms. *Too good*. As if she'd been running for a long time and someone had finally allowed her to stop and rest.

She found that she wanted to tell him. She wanted to explain about the other night.

'Lexie…*what*?'

She took a breath and then said starkly, 'I was raped when I was fourteen.'

Cesar went white in an instant. His whole body tensed. 'What did you say?' His voice was hoarse.

Lexie bit her lip. She couldn't go back now.

'I was raped by my aunt's husband. One night my parents and my aunt had gone out—he said he'd babysit. He brought me into my parents' room when the others were in bed and raped me.'

'The others…?'

'My five younger brothers and sisters.'

'*Dios mio*… Lexie…that animal…' Cesar looked sick. 'You looked at me the other night like I was going to hurt you—you were scared…'

Lexie leant forward and touched his arm. 'No…'

But Cesar was almost recoiling now, and she could see the horror on his face that she might have thought for a second he was capable of something so heinous.

She shook her head, '*No*, Cesar. I wasn't afraid of you. I knew this scene was coming up… I was apprehensive about it… It's the first time I've ever had to do a scene like this and it was just too close to the bone.'

Cesar pulled free of her touch and stood up, pacing again. Lexie was tense, her hands forming fists in her lap.

He faced her, eyes flinty green. 'My God,' he said again—in English this time.

Suddenly a kind of hurt bloomed inside her. He was looking at her as if she was a stranger. A damaged stranger. The guilt that she had worked long and hard to believe wasn't hers reared its ugly head again. Her rapist's accusations were as clear today as they had been then. *'You were asking for it, you know. Always prancing around under my nose dressed in that uniform.'*

She felt cold and said tightly, 'I'm sorry. I shouldn't have told you.'

She stood up from the couch, hating that she'd been weak enough to confide in Cesar. Hating that she'd thought his intuition made her feel as if he deserved to know.

'Where are you going?'

She looked at him. 'Back to my room.'

She turned and headed for the bedroom, but Cesar caught her hand. This time when she looked at him his eyes were blazing. 'Dammit, Lexie, you're staying here.'

Hot tears pricked the back of her eyes, galling her. She hadn't even cried after she'd been raped—too shocked and traumatised—and yet with one touch, one look, this man could reduce her to tears and make her want to lean on him when she'd fended for herself for so long now...

'Damn *you*, Cesar.' She pulled her hand free and faced him. 'Just let me go.'

He shook his head. 'You shouldn't be alone right now.'

More hurt bloomed inside Lexie to think that he was acting out of a sense of duty. 'I've done my therapy, Cesar, years of it,' she sneered. 'You really don't have to act as my babysitter just because it turns out that your lover is damaged goods.'

Now Cesar was angry. He took her arms in his hands, gripping her. 'Don't you *dare* put words in my mouth. I don't think any such thing. And you are *not* damaged. You're perfect.'

Lexie's anger drained away, leaving her feeling shaky. 'I'm sorry. I just…I shouldn't have told you.'

'I'm glad you told me. It's just a lot to take in.'

He let go of her arms and stepped back, raking a hand through his hair. Lexie felt bereft.

'Look,' she offered, 'I'm fine—really. I always suspected this scene would be difficult. But it's one of the reasons I took the job in the first place. Initially I wanted to say no, but I knew I couldn't let it stop me. I dealt with what happened a long time ago, Cesar. But something like this would be difficult even under the best of circumstances.'

Cesar shook his head lightly. He came close again, touched Lexie's jaw.

'You shouldn't have had to face it alone.'

Lexie felt emotion building inside her. Terrified of it, she said simply, 'I've always been alone.'

Cesar looked at her with a burning intensity. Desire, pure and hot, sparked to life within her, mixing with the emotion to produce something volatile. She brought her hand up to cover his and saw his eyes widen slightly.

'*Please…*'

One word. She could see that he understood, and she trembled inwardly in case he might balk. He could never know the depth of how badly she needed him right now— for myriad reasons.

His voice was gruff. 'Lexie…are you sure? The other night…'

She nodded. 'I'm sure. The other night…it wasn't about you. It was about me.'

'I don't want to hurt you.'

'You won't…'

He didn't move, though. Frustration welled inside her. Maybe Cesar couldn't deal with the ugly truth of what had happened to her. She took her hand down, stepped back, dislodging his hand. She'd just exposed herself spectacularly.

'It's okay… If you don't want me any more because of—'

His hand shot out, caught her. She looked at him.

'Of *course* I want you.' He sounded fierce. 'I just have to look at you to want you.'

He came closer. Held her face with both hands. 'You're in my blood. I need you.'

Lexie's own blood sang. She needed him too. Her whole being came alive as he drew her close and lowered his mouth to hers. The kiss was so tender and gentle that she almost emitted a sob of emotion, but held it back.

When he drew back he took her by the hand and led her into his bedroom. There was no sense of hesitation within Lexie. No sense of that same panic that had gripped her the other evening. She knew now that that had been largely because of her apprehension of acting out being raped. And it was over.

Cesar stopped by the bed and she faced him. He said, 'If you want to stop…'

Something melted inside her. She shook her head, her hands going to the buttons on his shirt, her voice husky with need. 'I won't want to stop.'

Her hands were clumsy on his buttons and he gently took them away to undo them himself. Lexie sucked in a breath to see his chest revealed. She opened the knot on her robe.

Cesar looked down and she saw a dark flush slash across his cheekbones. He slid his hands under the shoulders of her robe and pushed it till it fell to the floor.

Lexie ran her hands over his pectorals, her nails grazing his nipples, making them stand up into hard little points. She reached forward and put her mouth there, swirling her tongue around one hard tip, feeling her core moisten with desire.

As she lavished kisses on his chest and nipples her hands were on his jeans, flipping open the buttons, feeling the hard ridge of his arousal brushing her fingers. She drew back and pushed his jeans down, taking his underwear with them, her breath disappearing when his erection was freed.

She wrapped a hand around him, awed by his sheer size and strength and the knowledge that he would never use it to hurt her. Cesar was kicking his feet free of his clothes and then he put his hands on Lexie's arms.

She looked up.

He sounded rough. 'I need you. I need to taste you.'

Her hand stalled on the thick column of flesh and gently Cesar removed it, pushing her down onto the bed. He came down beside her and his mouth was on hers, and Lexie moaned as she tasted him hungrily, sucked him deep. Wrapped her legs and arms around him as if she could bind him to her for ever.

Gently Cesar unbound her, spreading her arms out, his mouth leaving hers to explore over her jaw and neck. Over the tops of her heaving breasts. Taking each tight bud of her nipples into his mouth, making her moan even louder and her hips writhe against him.

But he kept moving down, over her belly. An arm came under her back, arching her into him, his other hand pushed her legs apart.

She felt dizzy. 'Cesar...'

His green gaze was blistering. 'Trust me.'

Trust me. Lexie sank back. She did trust him. She always had—from the moment she'd met him and let him kiss her. *Her*—with her history. The knowledge rushed through her. Wiping aside any trepidation or lingering hurt.

His mouth was moving down, kissing the top of her

thigh. Moving in. A big hand was splayed under her buttocks, tipping her towards his face. Lexie's breaths were coming so hard and fast she had to consciously slow down for fear of passing out.

And then his tongue touched her *there*. He licked her with explicit skill. All the way up the seam of her body, his tongue delving into her secret folds, opening her up to him, baring every part of her.

Lexie's hands gripped the sheet. Legs bent, back arched. Cesar licked and sucked and drove her more and more mindless. His tongue swirled with maddening strokes against her clitoris before leaving it to lavish attention elsewhere and then returning just when those cells were screaming for release.

When it came it was so huge...so all-encompassing...that Lexie thought she'd passed out. Because the next thing she was aware of was Cesar sliding into her, so deeply and thoroughly, and with such a fierce look of concentration on his face that it was all she could do to wrap her legs around him as far as they'd go and tilt her hips to take him even deeper.

They were locked in a dance that was as old as time and as profound. Lexie couldn't look away from Cesar even though she felt as though her soul was being turned inside out and he'd see it as clear as day. *She loved him.* And it went deeper than just loving him because he was the first man she'd allowed herself to be intimate with. He was the *only* man she could imagine being intimate with. The only man she *wanted* to be intimate with.

That revelation came just as bliss split her body in two, throwing her high into the air, where she seemed to hang suspended on the crest of a huge wave until it finally dropped her again. Cesar caught her in his arms and rolled them both so that she went limp across his heaving chest, their hearts thundering in unison, their skin slick with perspiration.

* * *

In the aftermath of her shattering climax and revelation Lexie felt as wobbly and vulnerable as a new foal trying to stand on spindly legs. So much had happened, and in the past couple of days since leaving Cesar's apartment she'd deliberately cut herself off from the people around her, dreading the upcoming rape scene.

It had reminded her of when she'd arrived in London for the first time, when she'd been completely alone and unsupported.

Cesar shifted now and she winced minutely as the connection between their bodies was broken.

He asked with obvious concern, 'Are you okay?'

Lexie nodded and looked at him. He was on one elbow, some hair flopping into his forehead, his face dark, eyes glowing like dark green gems. *She loved him.*

But even as she knew that she also knew, with a feeling of desolation, that he didn't feel anything for her other than desire…and maybe worst of all pity.

Cutting into her thoughts, Cesar asked, 'What happened to him?'

Lexie went cold inside. 'My uncle?'

Cesar nodded.

She braced herself for the pain that inevitably came whenever he was mentioned or she thought about him, but it wasn't as sharp. Lexie's mouth became bitter. 'Nothing. My parents didn't want to know when I told them. They were very religious—pillars of the community. My father was a salesman; he travelled a lot. The thought of the scandal was too much for them.'

Cesar was incredulous. 'You mean he just got away with it?'

She pulled the sheet around her and sat up against the pillows. 'He died in a car crash about a year after it happened. But, no, he never got prosecuted or punished.'

'How could they have done that to you? Just ignored it?'

Lexie glanced away from Cesar. There was an even darker stain on her soul than he could imagine. She suddenly felt jaded and weary. Knowing that she loved him, but that it would end when she left the *castillo* for London at the end of that week, she felt reckless. As if she had nothing more to lose.

'That wasn't all,' she said now in a quiet voice.

'What do you mean?' Cesar moved, sitting up too.

She looked at him. 'The rape resulted in me becoming pregnant.'

He frowned. 'Pregnant? You had a baby?'

Lexie nodded, suppressing the inevitable spasm of emotion. 'A baby boy. I named him Connor.'

Cesar shook his head, clearly finding this hard to digest. 'But...you don't... Where is he now?'

'I had just turned fifteen when I had him. My family sent me away to a distant relative down the country for the duration of the pregnancy, where I was pretty much kept a prisoner for nine months. He was adopted two days after the birth, and is growing up somewhere in the greater Dublin area—that's all I know. And that they kept Connor as his middle name.'

Lexie watched as Cesar, looking slightly stunned, blindly pushed back the covers and got out of the bed. A sinking feeling gripped her. This was it. Her ugly truth bared. She'd known on some deep level that it would be too much to take in. This relationship was about a flirty affair while they were filming—not about dark secrets.

She knew with a sick feeling that she had just ended it.

CHAPTER TEN

CESAR PULLED ON his jeans and then he faced Lexie again. She looked impossibly young against the sheets, eyes huge. He was literally speechless. Didn't know what to say. The knowledge of what she'd been through was…enormous. And it was making all of his own dark demons rear their ugly heads.

He felt tight inside. As if a hand was closing around his chest and heart and squeezing with remorseless pressure. He thought of her reaction when he'd first presented her with the option of staying in the *castillo* for the duration of the shoot. No wonder she'd looked panicked.

Lexie was a mother. She'd had to give up her baby. He knew rationally that she'd had no choice, but it impacted on him in a deeply raw place. He couldn't breathe.

'Why did you tell me this?'

Lexie's eyes widened. Her face paled. And then something in her features hardened, as if in response to Cesar's stoniness.

'I told you because I felt I could… But I can see I shouldn't have.'

Cesar watched as if slightly removed from his own body as Lexie reached for her robe and pulled it on, getting out of bed too. Belting the robe tightly around her.

So many different emotions were impacting on him that it was almost overwhelming. Among them was anger—

which he knew was directed at himself, for his less than coherent response, and at Lexie for bringing him face to face with things he didn't want to look at in himself.

'I don't know what you want me to say.'

Lexie stared at him, her hair tumbled around her shoulders. Right then she seemed like a tiny warrior queen. Majestic.

'You don't have to say anything, Cesar. I'm not looking for therapy. I had years of that. I told you...'

She stopped for a second and that tightening sensation in Cesar's chest grew stronger. He almost put a hand there, as if that could alleviate the pain.

'I told you because I've never been with another man.'

Cesar stepped back. Stunned. 'Since you were...?'

Lexie snapped. 'Since I was raped, yes. You were my first lover.'

Faintly, Cesar said, 'Why me?'

She crossed her arms. 'You were the first man I desired.'

Lexie had never regretted anything more than opening her mouth to Cesar. Self-disgust ripped her insides to shreds. She'd truly learnt nothing. For a long time she'd felt ashamed, dirty. That she was some kind of damaged goods. And then therapy had helped her make sense of what had happened and she'd begun the long process of healing and forgiving herself.

Healing. The physical process of that, which had started with Cesar's incendiary kiss in the stable, mocked her now. She'd confused physical intimacy with something deeper. Clearly it had never been about anything else for him.

Her own family had shunned her a long time ago, and she was damned if she was going to let that happen again.

Lexie stalked around the bed and into the bathroom, aware of Cesar's eyes on her. The fact that he was so silent, not making any attempt to touch her, said it all. She closed the door and with shaking hands that told her of the heightened emotion she was barely reining in, she took off the robe and put on the costume nightshirt she'd been wearing for the rape scene.

When she emerged Cesar had put on a top. He looked serious.

Lexie hated that even now she was acutely aware of her sensitised naked body under the voluminous robe.

She was brisk. 'I shouldn't have said anything.' From somewhere, Lexie even managed to force a smile—as if this *hadn't* just cost her everything.

'Lexie—'

She cut him off, dreading hearing some platitude, and a spurt of anger made her say, 'Cesar, we're wrapping here on Friday. It's not as if this was ever going to go further. The papers have already lost interest in us—we've done what we set out to do in the first place.'

'We have.' His voice was flat.

'Yes,' Lexie insisted, forcing herself to look at him even though it was hard. 'I wanted to salvage my reputation and avoid being dragged through the tabloids again as some kind of victim. You wanted to avoid unnecessary scrutiny into your family. It was a mutually beneficial affair—isn't that what you called it?'

Everything within Cesar rejected Lexie's terse words but something was holding him back. The feeling that the very walls around him were about to start crumbling—as if some sort of invisible earthquake was happening below ground.

Right at that moment the full impact of just how different Lexie was from any other lover he'd had hit him with the force of a blunt object. She'd turned him upside down and inside out.

'Yes,' he agreed, 'it was.'

Just then there was a knock on the main door of Cesar's

apartment. He cursed even as a very weak part of him welcomed the interruption. He strode through the main living space to get to the door, and opened it to see one of the film's PAs.

'Sorry to disturb you, Mr Da Silva, but the director is looking for Lexie.'

Cesar knew Lexie was behind him without turning around. His skin prickled. He felt disorientated, dizzy. Even now he had to battle an absurd urge to protect her and snarl at the young guy to leave.

Lexie was oblivious to the messy tumult in Cesar's gut. She stepped around him, didn't look at him, and spoke to the PA. 'Tell Richard I'll just change before I come to him.'

The PA hurried off, clearly relieved to have delivered his message. Cesar watched Lexie. She was avoiding his eye. He wanted to tip her chin up, force her to meet his gaze, but at the same time he didn't want to see what was in those blue depths.

'I should go and talk to Richard.' Lexie's voice was husky, her almost belligerent stance of moments ago less evident.

She looked at him then and Cesar tensed, but her eyes were clear. Unreadable. It irritated him—which irritated him even more.

'The next few days are heavily scheduled so that we get out of here on time. I think it's best if we just…let this be finished now.'

Cesar felt slightly numb. This was a novel situation: a woman who was ready to walk away before he was ready to let her go.

Humiliation scored at his insides. Lexie was right—this had only ever been about the short term. The thought of anything beyond this place was not an option. He did not chase women around the world. Whatever desire he felt would dissipate. He could not want her so badly that he was unable to let her go.

He was tight-lipped as he reached for the door and held it open. 'Goodbye, Lexie.'

Something flared in her eyes for a second, and then it disappeared. She didn't speak again, just turned and walked out, and as Cesar watched her go he thought numbly that she could be a ghost in the long white gown and in her bare feet.

He closed the door on her, on that evocative image, and pushed down the chilling sensation that she would haunt him for ever. Everything he'd been holding in since she'd told him about the rape, and then the baby, surged up in a tangled black mess of emotion.

He went to his drinks cabinet and took out a glass, poured himself a drink. Taking a swift gulp, he felt the liquid jolt him back to life. His hand tightened on the glass as he stared unseeingly at the wall in front of him.

His own mother had abandoned him and left him at the mercy of his grandparents. Lexie had given up her own son. For a moment pure unadulterated rage rose up within Cesar as he acknowledged what she'd done —but it was an old, reflexive anger that had more to do with his mother than with Lexie.

His rage dimmed when he thought of Lexie aged fifteen, a terrified and traumatised schoolgirl. What choice had she had? None.

For the first time in his life Cesar had to concede that by the time his mother had come back for him his grandparents had done such a number on him that he'd had no choice but to reject her.

And he had to concede too that perhaps there had been more to his mother's motives than pure greed and selfishness. Her distress when she'd said goodbye both times stung him now—hard. Like a slap across the face. This unwelcome revelation brought with it an even stronger feeling that everything he'd always counted on was falling apart at the seams.

Cesar pinched the bridge of his nose. All he could see was Lexie's face and those huge eyes.

Anger surged again. What had she wanted from him? Damn her! Had she expected him to take her in his arms and soothe her? Promise her that everything would be all right?

Cesar wasn't gentle. Or sensitive. Or kind. He was black all the way through, and he resented Lexie right then for making him see just how black he was. For showing him how little he could offer comfort. And for making him think of the bleak reality of his childhood, filled with a lifetime of resentment for his two half-brothers. How powerless he'd been under the influence of his bitter grandparents, intent on punishment and revenge.

Rage and a feeling of impotence wound up inside him so tightly that he exploded. He turned and raised the hand holding that heavy crystal glass and with an inarticulate roar of pain and rage flung it with all his might across the room at his stainless steel kitchen. He watched it shatter into a million pieces, amber liquid spraying everywhere.

An echo from a long time ago whispered across his soul, bringing a chill wind. It reminded him that no good came out of this dark, gothic place. And to have imagined otherwise, even for a second, was to have become weak.

Lexie Anderson would be gone in a few days, and right in that moment Cesar hoped he'd never set eyes on her again. Because she'd done the worst thing in the world: she'd made him forget who he really was.

Lexie was sitting in her chair on the set, waiting while they set up for a new camera shot. People milled around her, working, chatting. But she felt removed. She'd heard the helicopter leaving early that morning.

She'd known that Cesar had left the *castillo* even before she'd heard one of the producers say something about him having business to attend to in America.

She'd been awake for most of the night, alternating between seething resentment directed at Cesar for having awoken her body from a lifetime of numbness and anger at herself for being so stupid as to fall for him. She'd tried to tell herself that she hadn't fallen so hard...but the hurt was too real and too deep for feelings not to be involved.

She'd never forget the look on his face when she'd told him about her baby. He'd shut down. Lexie had only ever talked about her baby to her counsellor. No one else knew. It was one of the reasons she was paranoid about press intrusion—in case anyone ever dug deep enough to find out.

Her son would be thirteen now, and every day Lexie wondered about him—wondered how she would cope if he ever came looking for her, asking for information. Sometimes the thought was overwhelming. She went cold inside as something struck her. Had she, on some level, put Cesar in the role of confidante because she'd been so desperate for support?

Even as Lexie felt anger for being so weak she had to acknowledge that she could have asked for help before. She'd just been too stubborn. That had been borne out the previous evening, when she'd gone to find the director to try and explain to him why she'd reacted the way she had.

She'd told him about the rape, knowing instinctively that she could trust him.

He'd shaken his head and taken her hand, his eyes full of compassion. 'Lexie, you should have told me. If I'd had any idea of how huge that scene was for you I'd have approached it differently. We could even have got it out of the way in the first week...'

He'd humbled her, apologising for unwittingly causing her distress. It was as if another weight had lifted from her shoulders, and Lexie knew that if she hadn't already told Cesar there was no way she could have confided in anyone else.

That only made her angry with him all over again. He hadn't been able to get rid of her fast enough yesterday. His face had been hard. Clearly he'd rejected her unwelcome confidences. No doubt his other lovers didn't come with messy histories, or weep all over him after making love.

She was glad Cesar was gone because she knew all her bravado was very shaky and that if she saw him again her heart would splinter into a million pieces.

Over a week later Cesar returned to the *castillo*. It was as if there had never been a film unit on the estate. Apart from the flattened bit of grass where the extras' marquee had stood everything had been restored to its pristine state— and, perversely, it annoyed Cesar intensely.

For the past week he'd put in long days at board meetings he'd been neglecting. Because of a blonde-haired, blue-eyed temptress. Damn her. Those were his favourite words at the moment, and they beat a constant refrain in his head.

Damn her for coming into his life. Damn her for making him want her so badly that he seemed to have a constant ache in his gut. Damn her for being so light in spite of the horrific things she'd endured.

Just...*damn her.*

For making him think of things like his brother Alexio's wedding and how happy both his half-brothers had looked with their wives. And damn her for making him come to the uncomfortable realisation that he had to stop blaming his brothers for living their lives oblivious of his presence.

That realisation had hit him as he'd looked blearily into

the bottom of an empty bottle of whiskey in a dingy bar on the Lower East Side of Manhattan about two days ago.

Cesar stopped at the entrance of the *castillo*. It sat there, as forbidding and dark as it ever had been. But for the first time in his life it didn't feel quite so…oppressive.

It was quiet, though. And that quiet, which had never really bothered him before, seemed to reach around him and squeeze, bringing with it restlessness. Dissatisfaction.

Without even being aware of making the decision, Cesar found himself walking up the main staircase to the first-floor landing. He went and stood at the window where his grandmother had found him waiting, looking for his mother.

He felt the old pain like a bruise that would never fade. But it didn't bring with it that futile sense of anger. It only brought a sense of melancholy and a growing sense of something else. *Loss*. Acute, aching loss. Worse than anything he'd ever felt before—worse even the loss he could remember feeling as a child for his mother.

Cesar knew then that as much as his grandparents had all but imprisoned him in this *castillo* when he was a child, since he'd become an adult he'd happily inflicted the same punishment on himself, and self-disgust filled him.

Lexie's face and eyes filled his vision. How she'd looked that last time he'd seen her, in the ridiculous period night-gown. Pale. Yet strong. Defiant in the face of his frankly pathetic response to her pain and trauma.

Something had shut down inside him that day, as if to protect him from feeling the pain too acutely. But now that was breaking apart inside him as he stared out at a bleak view that was seared into his consciousness.

He was sick of bleak. He was sick of darkness. He was sick of himself.

Damn Lexie, indeed. Because she hadn't made him

forget who he was at all. She'd shown him *exactly* who he was and who he could be. If he was brave enough.

The street was stinking, narrow. Beggars lined it, calling out for mercy or money. Small children darted under people's feet. Lexie stepped out of the path of a horse and carriage only at the last moment and gasped as it whistled past. Her long skirts were splashed with mud. People jostled her. She was going against the tide. And all she could think about, even as the cameras were running, was *him*. Cesar.

She cursed him for about the hundredth time that day and hoped that her expression conveyed anger at her co-star, who followed her through the streets, tracking her like a hunted animal.

'Cut!'

Immediately Lexie stopped. All of the extras turned and went back to their first positions on the enormous set that had been built for the film on a back lot in the London studios. A swarm of crew moved in to rearrange things, fix focus marks, touch up hair and make-up.

Lexie felt removed, though. The director approached her and she smiled brightly.

He took her arm and said in a low voice, 'Lexie, are you all right? You just seem…not that focused.'

She grimaced inwardly, regretting having ever told him what had happened to her. He'd been overly solicitous ever since. 'Sorry, Richard… I'm fine. It's just—'

'Oh, my God.'

'Sir! *Sir!* You can't go onto the set without a pass!'

Richard frowned and looked past Lexie. 'What on earth is *he* doing here?' he said incredulously.

Lexie felt a prickling sensation and turned around to see a tall figure approaching them. But even now she couldn't really compute that it was *him*.

Cesar. Dressed in dark worn jeans. A jumper and a battered brown leather jacket. Dark golden hair glinting in the London sunshine. He was almost too gorgeous to be real.

She even heard one of the extras nearby say in an awe-struck voice, 'Who *is* that?' and Lexie could almost sympathise with the inevitable impact he would be having on some poor unsuspecting person's senses.

He looked as intense as she'd ever seen him. A security guard caught up with him and took his arm. Cesar shook him off and kept coming.

Her mouth had gone bone-dry. She wondered if she was seeing things. Damn this corset that constricted her breath...

Cesar stopped just feet away and the security guard came panting up behind him. 'Now, look here—'

Lexie put out a shaky hand. 'It's all right, we know him. I...know him.'

Then all the anger and pain that had been her constant companion for a week now came flooding up, boiling over. She hissed at Cesar, 'What are you doing here? We're in the middle of a scene.'

'So I see,' he remarked dryly, taking in all the gawping extras and the crew, who were loving the interruption. He looked back at Lexie, and then spoke as if they were continuing a conversation that had stopped only moments ago. 'The thing is I should never have agreed with you when you said we should end the affair.'

Lexie gulped and darted a look at the avid crowd. 'Cesar, do we really have to do this here?'

Just then Richard stepped forward. 'Now, listen, Da Silva—interrupting my set once was—'

Cesar took his eyes off Lexie to stare at the man, and Lexie shivered when she saw the familiar steel in his expression.

'How much will it cost to shut down production for the rest of the day?'

Lexie blinked. Richard spluttered. 'I'd have to ask the producer...'

'Well, why don't you find him and ask him, and whatever amount he gives you tell him I'll double it.'

A murmur started through the crew and the extras. Lexie could see the PAs galvanised into action at the thought of an early wrap and a day off. The set started to clear.

Cesar stepped right up to Lexie and she was rooted to the spot. Terrified of the flutters that had started in her belly. Her heart squeezed. She loved this man so much, but he'd hurt her, and if all he wanted was to continue their affair...

'Cesar, if you've come just because you're not ready to end the affair then I'm not interested.'

His gaze on hers became assessing. Lexie's body hummed with awareness. With hunger.

'So what *are* you interested in?'

She blinked, confused. Fear gripped her... *What had she just said?* 'I just told you—I'm not interested in an affair.'

A ghost of a smile touched Cesar's mouth and she realised very belatedly how dishevelled he was, with stubble lining his jaw.

'One thing I do know is that I am not ready to end the affair—and I don't think you are either.'

A ball of pain lodged in her gut. She didn't have it in her to keep seeing Cesar knowing that it would end. Even one night with this man would kill her, even though every cell in her body was crying out for his touch.

She stepped back, her movement slightly hampered by her long dress. 'Yes, I am. And you should go and tell Richard you were joking about shutting down the production before too many people leave. You've caused enough disruption in my life as it is.'

Lexie went to walk around him, cursing her costume when she couldn't move more freely.

Cesar caught her and whirled her around, eyes flashing. 'I've caused disruption in *your* life? What about the disruption you've caused *me*?' He pointed a finger at his chest and glared at her.

Lexie pulled free, her anger matching his, boiling over when she thought of how naive she'd been, baring her soul to him.

'I did nothing but warm your bed for a few weeks! I was a convenient lover who also handily deflected some heat from the press about your family issues, and you were quite happy to take advantage of that.'

'On the contrary—you weren't *convenient* at all! The fact is, Lexie Anderson, you have been the most singularly *in*convenient lover I've ever known.'

Cesar was practically roaring now, and Lexie's eyes stung with tears. She bit back the lump in her throat to hear Cesar declare so baldly just how much he resented his desire for her.

Her voice was thick. 'Well, then, what are you waiting for? Leave me be.'

She went to walk away before Cesar could see the extent of her distress, but he caught her again. She cursed out loud, but he had both hands on her arms now.

Lexie felt a tear slip down one cheek and cursed again, struggling against his hold. She stopped and looked up. 'Just...let me go, Cesar. Please. I can't do this.'

He paled under his dark skin. 'I didn't want to make you cry.' His hands tightened. 'The reason you were an inconvenient lover is because you made me face up to myself in a way no one ever has before. Or will again.'

Now Cesar looked almost angry, but something in Lexie went very still.

'I was doing just fine without anyone challenging my

emotionally barren life. And then *you* appeared, literally like some kind of vision, and from that moment on something broke inside me. Something that needed to be broken.'

Cesar moved his hands up to cup Lexie's jaw.

'The truth is that you were…you *are*…the most beautifully *necessary* inconvenience, because you've brought me back to life. I don't want to end the affair, Lexie—*ever*. I want it to last for the rest of our lives.'

Lexie tried to shake her head, as if that might improve her hearing. But Cesar's hands held her immobile. She had to put her hands out to touch him, barely able to breathe. 'What are you saying?'

The tendrils of something impossibly light and effervescent were scaring her, beckoning her to a place where surely she would face the most epic fall of all if she was dreaming this.

'What I'm saying is that I'm in love with you. I think I have been from the moment I saw you. And I want to spend the rest of my life with you. I want it all—the picket fence, children, even the damn dog. *Everything.*'

His mouth twisted.

'When you asked me about getting married I taunted you because I couldn't bear the fact that you'd put a seed of something incredibly fragile in my head. A hope for the future I'd never even allowed myself to think about or imagine.'

Emotion was blooming inside Lexie's chest, making it expand, making her dizzy. She wanted to laugh and cry at the same time. But then she remembered his stark non-reaction that day at the *castillo*. The way he'd let her go so easily.

One of her hands on Cesar's chest curled into a fist and she hit him ineffectually. Her voice was choked. 'You hurt me. I thought you didn't care.'

Cesar looked pained. 'I'm so sorry—my response was... pathetic. I cared so much I shut down. I literally didn't know what to do or say. You were telling me those things... and all I could feel was my own pain. I couldn't begin to understand the horror of what had happened to you. I wanted to go out and find that man and kill him with my bare hands.'

Lexie paled.

'For the last week I've kept imagining you as a young girl, alone and scared, going through pregnancy and birth without any support.' He shook his head, his eyes glittering a little too brightly. 'You're the bravest person I know. You humble me.'

'I thought...' Lexie was whispering now '...that you hated what I'd told you because it was too personal. And that you didn't understand why I had to do what I did. I thought afterwards that it must have reminded you of your mother.'

Cesar's thumb caressed her cheek. 'If anything it's helped me to understand her a little better, because it's not so black and white any more. She wouldn't have been human if she hadn't felt some pain on leaving me behind— and God knows what nefarious bargain my grandparents struck with her to make her stay away.'

Feeling absurdly shy, Lexie said, 'I thought you resented the fact that I'd told you those things because our relationship wasn't about anything but...sex.'

Cesar grimaced. 'At first I did. I was angry because you'd forced me to acknowledge that what I felt for you went a lot deeper than I'd admitted to myself.'

Lexie could see it on his face now—in his eyes. Love. Blasting her doubts and fears. But it was huge. She was scared.

As if he could tell, he moved even closer and said throatily, 'What is it?'

'I'm scared,' she whispered, baring herself in a way she'd never done with anyone before. 'I'm scared because my own family turned their backs on me. Betrayed me in the worst possible way. I couldn't survive that again.'

Lexie could feel the tension in Cesar's body, see the ferocity in his expression.

'I vow to you with every breath in my body that I will spend my life protecting you from hurt and harm. I love you, Lexie. You're as much a part of my soul as I am myself. A betrayal of you is a betrayal of me...and whatever the future brings I'm going to be right by your side to deal with it. Including Connor.'

Lexie's eyes filled with tears. The fact that he'd acknowledged her son dissolved the last of her defences.

Cesar was blurry in her vision as she came up on tiptoe and slid her arms around his neck. 'I love you, Cesar... so much.'

He groaned softly and covered her mouth with his. The kiss was searing and passionate.

Lexie broke free and looked up. 'Take me home, please?'

Cesar smiled and his thumbs wiped away the tracks of her tears on her cheeks. '*Espere querida*...wait... There's just one thing I have to do first.'

Suddenly Cesar disappeared, and Lexie gave a little surprised yelp to see him kneeling at her feet, her huge skirt between them. He was holding out a black box which he then opened. He looked up, his slightly nervous smile making Lexie's heart flip-flop.

'Lexie Anderson...will you marry me?'

More tears filled Lexie's eyes. Pure joy bubbled up inside her. Her heart was in her voice when she said simply, 'Yes!'

Cesar took her hand and slid a stunning antique gold and diamond ring on her finger. The fact that she'd barely looked at it didn't seem to bother either of them, because he stood up and swept her and her voluminous dress into his arms before kissing her senseless—much to the entertainment of the security guards, who were the only people left on the set.

A week later Cesar had arranged to have his private jet standing by at a nearby private airfield. As soon as Lexie was wrapped after her final scene later that day they were going back to Spain.

Cesar's mobile phone beeped with a message and he read it.

Congratulations on your engagement. Alexio and I would like to meet you, if you're ready. Call me any time. Rafaele.

Cesar showed the message to Lexie later, when they were on the plane, and she was sitting in his lap. She looked at him and he saw the way her eyes grew suspiciously bright.

She pressed a kiss to his cheek and said, 'I'm ready when you are.'

Incredible joy gripped him—there wasn't a hint of the old darkness and pain. Cesar grinned and threw his phone down, and then got busy showing his fiancée just how ready he was.

EPILOGUE

Eighteen months later

'I MEAN…THEY look so innocent, don't they?'

Cesar smiled at Alexio's almost incredulous tone. Rafaele sighed deeply on his other side. They'd been standing and talking and were now watching the three women who were sitting around a picnic table under a huge tree, a few yards away. They were on Cesar's lawn, at the back of the *castillo*, where a new outdoor pool twinkled invitingly through some small trees.

The *castillo* looked the same on the outside but it had been almost completely remodelled on the inside, so that very few vestiges of the past remained apart from the parts that had to be preserved. It was light and airy, with vast spaces, and decorated with a sumptuous yet understated luxury. Lexie had personally supervised the storage of the portraits of Cesar's grandparents in a special airtight room deep in the cellars.

'I know,' Rafaele said now. 'And yet in spite of that innocence they all—

'Brought us down,' Cesar chipped in, sounding the happiest out of all of them.

Just then the three women's heads drew closer together: one dark, one bright blonde and the other reddish blonde. There came a very distinctive peal of laughter from Samantha Falcone, and then they were all guffawing inelegantly, heads thrown back.

Rafaele shifted uncomfortably. 'Why does that always make me nervous? As if they're talking—

'About us?' Alexio cut in.

'Because they probably are,' Cesar said equably, once again sounding like a Zen Buddha.

His younger half-brothers turned towards him and folded their arms, two versions of his own green eyes narrowed on him.

Alexio remarked dryly, 'I could take a photo of you right now and Tweet it and you'd lose your well-honed mystique in seconds.'

Cesar smiled and said ruefully, 'Be my guest. I think I lost that mystique somewhere around the first nappy-change, when my sense of smell got scarred for life.'

The tiny bundle wriggled against his chest and he looked down at the small downy head of his two-month-old daughter, Lucita, where she was burrowing into a more comfortable position. His hand supported her bottom in the baby sling protectively.

Just then a small toddler in a bright dress broke free of the women at the table and tottered towards the men with a determined expression on her face. A halo of strawberry-blond ringlets framed a heart-stoppingly cherubic face dominated by huge green eyes.

She'd already wrapped everyone within a ten-mile radius around her tiny finger—even Cesar's normally very taciturn housekeeper.

Cesar's chest grew tight as he imagined Lucita at that age. And growing older in a vastly different *castillo* from the one he'd experienced. One filled with light and love.

Alexio bent down and encouraged his daughter Belle the last few yards, until she fell into his arms with a squeal of excitement. Lifting her up, he settled her high against his chest, a distinctly soppy expression on his face as she rested her head between his neck and shoulder, thumb firmly in her mouth.

'How the mighty are fallen indeed,' Rafaele remarked wryly, observing this just as Milo, his almost five-year-old son, streaked by with his armbands on, ready to jump into the pool, followed swiftly by Juan Cortez's similarly aged son—Milo's new best friend.

Belle immediately straightened up to take her thumb from her mouth and pointed a clutching hand at where Milo was, exclaiming urgently in baby gibberish.

But Alexio's attention was fixated on his wife, Sidonie, who had followed her daughter and was sliding an arm around her husband's waist. She wore a long colourful kaftan over a bikini.

Cesar knew that they were sitting on the news that they were expecting again until Sidonie had passed three months. But Sid had already told Lexie, and Lexie had told Cesar, and he was pretty sure that Sam must know too—which meant Rafaele knew, which meant it was an open secret. But of course no one would acknowledge it till they did.

The look between Alexio and Sidonie was definitely carnal and very private.

She smiled as Belle wriggled to be put down. 'You know that now she's seen Milo she won't rest until she can play with him.'

Alexio scowled in Rafaele's direction and Rafaele raised a brow. 'What? It's not *my* fault she's hero-worshipping her cousin. She's displaying remarkably good taste in men already. That's a *good* thing!'

Sidonie just shook her head at the men's ribbing and took Belle's hand when Alexio let her down. She glanced fondly at where her new niece was cuddled against Cesar's chest. 'Lucita's due a feed, and Sam wants to take a nap, so I said I'd watch the kids. I'll take Belle to the pool.'

Alexio immediately declared, 'I'll come too,' and another hot, private look passed between them.

Samantha Falcone was walking towards them now, still graceful despite her seven months pregnant belly, evident under a stretchy dress. When she came near Rafaele drew her close and asked throatily, 'You're taking a nap?'

She looked up at him and nodded, and then said, far too innocently, 'You didn't sleep very well last night, did you? Maybe you should take a nap too?'

Cesar almost laughed out loud at the way Rafaele muttered something unintelligble and all but dragged his pregnant wife into the *castillo*. Rafaele had confided that this time was very poignant for him, because he'd missed Sam's pregnancy with Milo.

Alexio and Sidonie were now wandering off hand in hand, with Belle toddling in front of them, towards the pool.

Cesar looked over to where Lexie sat on the love seat beneath the tree, watching him. She smiled and crooked her finger. As if he needed any encouragement…

When he sat down beside her Lucita was already raising her head and mewling softly, clearly ready for her feed.

Deftly Cesar unhooked the sling and lifted his daughter out, holding her head securely as her huge blue eyes opened wide and she gazed back at him guilelessly. His heart clenched. Was it possible to fall even more deeply in love every time he looked at her? And then she smiled and the question became moot, because he fell fathoms deeper in a nanosecond.

'Look!' Cesar declared proudly, angling her for Lexie's inspection. 'She smiled at me.'

Lexie grinned and took their daughter from his safe

hands, settling her against the breast she'd bared, helping that seeking mouth to find her nipple.

As Lucita latched on, Lexie said wryly, 'I hate to burst your bubble but it's probably just wind.'

Cesar said nothing and when she peeked at him he was just smiling at her, a very private smile. He put his arm around her and said throatily, 'I could watch you nurse Lucita all day.'

Lexie rested her head back against him and smiled. 'Happy?'

Cesar looked down at her and felt his heart swell so much it might explode. Those huge blue eyes sucked him in as they had that very first time.

He shook his head and said quickly, '*Happy* doesn't even come close to how I'm feeling.'

He took Lexie's free hand—the hand on which she wore his rings. He brought it up and pressed his mouth there, over the rings that bound them together for ever.

He found himself admitting something he'd been too ashamed to admit before. 'Do you know…just before Lucita was born I was afraid…afraid that I couldn't possibly love any more than I already loved you?'

Lexie's eyes grew bright.

'But as soon as she was born I realised it's infinite. Love can't be bound to one person.'

'I know,' Lexie whispered. 'I felt it too.'

The pregnancy and birth had been incredibly emotional for them both, but especially poignant for Lexie, considering it had brought back everything she'd been through with her first baby. But Cesar had been with her every step of the way, and more supportive than she might have dared to imagine. With his encouragement she'd even been in touch with the adoption agency to leave word as to where she could be contacted should her son ever feel the desire.

A deep sense of peace and security pervaded her life now. And love.

Lexie huffed a small laugh then, even as emotional tears made her eyes glitter. 'You know, for someone who was deprived of love growing up you're remarkably good at it.'

Cesar smiled back and said, with not a little sadness, 'I can feel sorry for my grandparents now. They were so bitter and caught up in anger.'

Predictably, at the mention of his grandparents, Lexie's eyes flashed with emotion. But before it could rise Cesar pressed a kiss to Lexie's mouth, long and lingering, full of love.

When he drew back the fire of anger had gone out of Lexie's eyes to be replaced by another kind of fire, and she said, almost grumpily, 'That was blatant distraction.'

Lucita's mouth popped free and Lexie handed her back to Cesar while she prepared her other breast for feeding.

When their daughter had emitted a gratifyingly robust burp Cesar handed her back. With Lucita settled again, Lexie looked at her husband. 'Are you ready for tomorrow?'

'Tomorrow?' he asked disingenuously, clearly much more interested in his wife and baby. 'Tell me what's happening tomorrow again?'

Lexie smiled. He knew exactly what was happening. Even so, she reminded him. 'Sidonie's aunt is arriving and it's her first time out of France, so we all have to be very mindful of her. Alexio is going to Paris to meet her and bring her here so she won't be nervous. Rafaele's father and his new wife Bridie are coming from Milan. And Juan Cortez and Maria are coming to pick up Miguel— although you know they'll probably end up spending the night because it'd be rude not to ask them to stay for the barbecue...'

'And,' added Cesar dryly, 'because Maria is as thick as thieves with you and Sid and Sam.'

Lexie smiled, but couldn't stem a niggle of anxiety for Cesar. This was their biggest family get-together yet. And it would getting bigger all the time—especially as Sam's new baby would be born soon and added to the mix. And then Sid's.

It had been easier for Lexie, knowing what it was to come from a sizeable family, in spite of their estrangement. And also because she and Sam and Sidonie had formed a solid and genuine friendship almost within the first ten minutes of meeting each other.

She knew that even though Cesar's relationship with his half-brothers had taken a quantum leap ever since that first meeting in Rome, when she'd gone with him to meet them properly for the first time, it was still a novel experience for him to play at happy families having come from the exact opposite experience.

But then, it had been healing for Cesar to hear how Rafaele and Alexio had suffered at the hands of their unhappy mother in their own lives. Happy families didn't come naturally to them either. Once he'd seen they could empathise with him he hadn't felt so alone in his experiences.

Lexie saw the glint of determination in Cesar's eyes and castigated herself for underestimating how he might deal with this. He pressed another lingering kiss to her mouth and then pulled back, saying with a grin that transformed him into someone infinitely younger and even more gorgeous, 'Am I ready? As long as you're with me I'm ready for anything.'

Lexie answered huskily, with her heart in her voice, 'Well, that's easy—because I'm not going anywhere.'

* * * * *

ROMANCE

Ravelli's Defiant Bride	Lynne Graham
When Da Silva Breaks the Rules	Abby Green
The Heartbreaker Prince	Kim Lawrence
The Man She Can't Forget	Maggie Cox
A Question of Honour	Kate Walker
What the Greek Can't Resist	Maya Blake
An Heir to Bind Them	Dani Collins
Playboy's Lesson	Melanie Milburne
Don't Tell the Wedding Planner	Aimee Carson
The Best Man for the Job	Lucy King
Falling for Her Rival	Jackie Braun
More than a Fling?	Joss Wood
Becoming the Prince's Wife	Rebecca Winters
Nine Months to Change His Life	Marion Lennox
Taming Her Italian Boss	Fiona Harper
Summer with the Millionaire	Jessica Gilmore
Back in Her Husband's Arms	Susanne Hampton
Wedding at Sunday Creek	Leah Martyn

MEDICAL

200 Harley Street: The Soldier Prince	Kate Hardy
200 Harley Street: The Enigmatic Surgeon	Annie Claydon
A Father for Her Baby	Sue MacKay
The Midwife's Son	Sue MacKay

Mills & Boon® Large Print
June 2014

ROMANCE

A Bargain with the Enemy	Carole Mortimer
A Secret Until Now	Kim Lawrence
Shamed in the Sands	Sharon Kendrick
Seduction Never Lies	Sara Craven
When Falcone's World Stops Turning	Abby Green
Securing the Greek's Legacy	Julia James
An Exquisite Challenge	Jennifer Hayward
Trouble on Her Doorstep	Nina Harrington
Heiress on the Run	Sophie Pembroke
The Summer They Never Forgot	Kandy Shepherd
Daring to Trust the Boss	Susan Meier

HISTORICAL

Portrait of a Scandal	Annie Burrows
Drawn to Lord Ravenscar	Anne Herries
Lady Beneath the Veil	Sarah Mallory
To Tempt a Viking	Michelle Willingham
Mistress Masquerade	Juliet Landon

MEDICAL

From Venice with Love	Alison Roberts
Christmas with Her Ex	Fiona McArthur
After the Christmas Party...	Janice Lynn
Her Mistletoe Wish	Lucy Clark
Date with a Surgeon Prince	Meredith Webber
Once Upon a Christmas Night...	Annie Claydon

0514 GEN STD LP

Mills & Boon® Hardback

July 2014

ROMANCE

Christakis's Rebellious Wife	Lynne Graham
At No Man's Command	Melanie Milburne
Carrying the Sheikh's Heir	Lynn Raye Harris
Bound by the Italian's Contract	Janette Kenny
Dante's Unexpected Legacy	Catherine George
A Deal with Demakis	Tara Pammi
The Ultimate Playboy	Maya Blake
Socialite's Gamble	Michelle Conder
Her Hottest Summer Yet	Ally Blake
Who's Afraid of the Big Bad Boss?	Nina Harrington
If Only...	Tanya Wright
Only the Brave Try Ballet	Stefanie London
Her Irresistible Protector	Michelle Douglas
The Maverick Millionaire	Alison Roberts
The Return of the Rebel	Jennifer Faye
The Tycoon and the Wedding Planner	Kandy Shepherd
The Accidental Daddy	Meredith Webber
Pregnant with the Soldier's Son	Amy Ruttan

MEDICAL

200 Harley Street: The Shameless Maverick	Louisa George
200 Harley Street: The Tortured Hero	Amy Andrews
A Home for the Hot-Shot Doc	Dianne Drake
A Doctor's Confession	Dianne Drake

0614GEN STD HB

Mills & Boon® Large Print

July 2014

ROMANCE

A Prize Beyond Jewels	Carole Mortimer
A Queen for the Taking?	Kate Hewitt
Pretender to the Throne	Maisey Yates
An Exception to His Rule	Lindsay Armstrong
The Sheikh's Last Seduction	Jennie Lucas
Enthralled by Moretti	Cathy Williams
The Woman Sent to Tame Him	Victoria Parker
The Plus-One Agreement	Charlotte Phillips
Awakened By His Touch	Nikki Logan
Road Trip with the Eligible Bachelor	Michelle Douglas
Safe in the Tycoon's Arms	Jennifer Faye

HISTORICAL

The Fall of a Saint	Christine Merrill
At the Highwayman's Pleasure	Sarah Mallory
Mishap Marriage	Helen Dickson
Secrets at Court	Blythe Gifford
The Rebel Captain's Royalist Bride	Anne Herries

MEDICAL

Her Hard to Resist Husband	Tina Beckett
The Rebel Doc Who Stole Her Heart	Susan Carlisle
From Duty to Daddy	Sue MacKay
Changed by His Son's Smile	Robin Gianna
Mr Right All Along	Jennifer Taylor
Her Miracle Twins	Margaret Barker

Discover more romance at

www.millsandboon.co.uk

- ❤ WIN great prizes in our exclusive competitions

- ❤ BUY new titles before they hit the shops

- ❤ BROWSE new books and REVIEW your favourites

- ❤ SAVE on new books with the Mills & Boon® Bookclub™

- ❤ DISCOVER new authors

PLUS, to chat about your favourite reads, get the latest news and find special offers:

- 📘 Find us on facebook.com/millsandboon
- 🐦 Follow us on twitter.com/millsandboonuk
- ❤ Sign up to our newsletter at millsandboon.co.uk